CIARAN CARSON wa[...] author of four prose works. [...] *Fishing for Amber*, and *Shamrock Tea*, which was long-listed for the Booker Prize. A novel, *The Pen Friend*, was published in 2009. He is the author of ten collections of poetry, including *Belfast Confetti*, which won the *Irish Times*/Aer Lingus Award for Irish Poetry, the Ewart-Biggs Prize, the Irish Book Award and was shortlisted for the Whitbread Prize; *First Language*, which won the T.S. Eliot Prize; and *Breaking News*, which won the Forward Poetry Prize. *Collected Poems* was published in 2008, and a book of verse translations of Rimbaud's prose poems, *In the Light Of*, in 2012. *The Táin*, his translation of the Old Irish epic, was published in 2007. Carson lives in Belfast and is the director of the Seamus Heaney Centre for Poetry at Queen's University. He is a member of Aosdána.

First published in 2012 by Blackstaff Press
4c Heron Wharf
Sydenham Business Park
Belfast BT3 9LE
with the assistance of
The Arts Council of Northern Ireland

The acknowledgements on pages 207–208 constitute an
extension of this copyright page.

Typeset by CJWT Solutions, St Helens, Merseyside

Printed in Great Britain by the MPG Books Group

A CIP catalogue for this book is available
from the British Library

ISBN 978 085640 903 5

www.blackstaffpress.com

EXCHANGE PLACE
CIARAN CARSON

BLACKSTAFF PRESS

For Terry and Tara

INTRODUCTION

It begins or began with a missing notebook, an inexpensive Muji A6 notebook with buff card covers and feint-ruled pages. On the inside cover is written, If found, please return to John Kilfeather, 41 Elsinore Gardens, Belfast BT15 3FB, Northern Ireland, United Kingdom, Europe, The World. It is one of a series of such notebooks in which I have written or scribbled over the years: notes for a book I intend to write, random observations, titles of books I have read or intend to read, quotations from books or journals I have read or skimmed, snippets of conversation overheard in bars or on buses. Lists of words. Each notebook is a record of a journey which begins without my knowing where I am going, or where I will end up. Here and there are names and addresses of people I have met on the way, sometimes in their own handwriting, sometimes in mine, which varies from near-illegible scrawl to near-calligraphic script, depending on my mood, or, to tell the truth, whatever mood-altering substance I might have taken before taking up the pen. But more of that anon.

Every so often I sift through the notebooks and carefully write up selected passages into larger, A5 Muji notebooks, editing as I go, trying to make sense of what has been written. I am writing these words in such a notebook. Many notebooks, whether A6 or A5, remain unfilled as my train of thought takes another turn and I begin another notebook, turning over a new leaf as it were. I have just opened one at this passage, transcribed from a *Times Educational Supplement*, dated 20/12/02. 'The library angel,' it reads, 'is a recognised phenomenon, but only by those who have encountered it. You enter a library, in search of information; you have no idea where to begin looking, and yet something directs you to a particular shelf, to take down a particular book, for no good reason as far as you can tell, but it turns out to be the very book you need.' As it is, the particular A6 notebook I think I need is missing. I want this notebook because I think it contains a passage which I might well use as part of the larger narrative scheme I have in mind. It might even provide a key.

I look for the notebook in the drawers of the desk where I am writing this. I look through my bookshelves, for I have a habit of lodging notebooks in between books, books from which I have transcribed passages into the notebooks, or books which I think relevant to the writing in hand. I look in the filing cabinet. I go through the pockets of my many jackets, which hang in several wardrobes in several rooms of the house. For the present, the notebook remains missing. But I imagine it in my hands, leafing through it until I find the passage I am looking for, written a year or two or three ago under the awning of the Morning Star. I had arranged to meet a client in Muriel's bar round the corner, but I like to arrive some thirty minutes early to relax by myself with a smoke and a drink, and the tiny al fresco smoking area of Muriel's was full. Besides, the pleasant afternoon had clouded over suddenly; thunder was in the air. So I proceeded to the Morning Star for the time being. I sat at one of the trestle tables under the large striped awning. A young waiter took my order for a Pernod with ice and water, and I rolled a cigarette. As I did so I glanced at the only other customer in the area, sitting two tables away from me. He reminded me of someone. I lit the cigarette, took out my notebook, and began to write. I had written a page or two, and, pen poised, was about to write more when there was a flash of lightning followed by an almighty thunderclap and it began to pour rain, stair-rods of it drumming on the awning, and a gust of wind carried a flurry of raindrops on to the open notebook, spattering the words I had written in Waterman's blue-black ink with a vintage Waterman's Ideal fountain pen. I remember thinking that this was some kind of sign or other. I moved to a more sheltered spot, and scribbled down some more words. What I wrote then remains to be seen. It occurred to me to search the attic.

I'm standing there now, dismayed by the heaps of books, clothes, shoes, boots, picture frames, boxes of bric-a-brac or junk, cardboard files, boxes of cassette tapes, broken lamps, a scale model Spitfire aeroplane, a toy Luger pistol, an ancient word-processor, a Land camera, broken clocks, all covered in a layer of dust; I haven't been up here in months. I pick up an unlabelled box-file, blow off the dust, and open it. It contains a typescript. The first page bears the title $X+Y=K$. To say that I had forgotten entirely about it would be an exaggeration; but it had been pushed well to the back of my mind for a long time. It is a draft of a book I wrote some years ago and then abandoned. As I skim it, bits of it are familiar; others seem written by someone else. How much of ourselves we forget.

Here, for example, was a passage I recognized as having been lifted from the work of the French philosopher Henri Bergson:

'There is no perception which is not permeated with memories. With the immediate and present data of our senses we mingle a thousand details out of our past experience. In most cases these memories supplant our actual perceptions, of which we then retain only a few hints, thus using them as signs that recall to us former images. The convenience and the rapidity of perception is bought at this price; but hence also springs every kind of illusion.'

And here, another passage obviously shadowing the writing of another author, whose name I could not remember, no doubt originally scrawled in a notebook somewhere: 'The city is a living organism, infected by a swarm of microbe-like practices which government was supposed to administer or suppress. But, far from being regulated or eliminated by a panoptic administration, these elements have proceeded to insinuate themselves into the networks of surveillance, reaching an accommodation which is merely concealed by the frantic discourses of the observational establishment. Bugs proliferate. Drop ceiling air spaces, closets, crawl spaces, air ducts, cavity walls, all heavily infiltrated by a variety of listening devices nominally employed by one side or the other.'

I realize I might have to reread the whole book to understand this passage fully, or what I might have meant by it. But as I skim $X+Y=K$ I begin to see that some of its concerns are my concerns now: perception, memory, identity, surveillance, disappearances and appearances. And it seems I might be able to recycle some of this material – plagiarizing myself, as it were – in this other book that has been at the back of my mind for some years, as yet unwritten, for which I thought the missing notebook might provide a key. Perhaps this other book is the book I meant to write then. It concerns an erstwhile close friend, let us call him John Harland, who disappeared without trace from my life some years ago, without so much as a by-your-leave. I am still trying to figure out why.

1

THE FOUND WATCH

Like most citizens of Belfast who have lived through the Troubles, I have learned to be wary. I look and listen, since you never know who might be watching or listening in on you. And, as a dealer, I have learned to look at things all the more closely. I can scan a market stall and, in a matter of seconds, home in on the gold among the dross: the unprepossessing little cup that turns out to be Meissen; the grimy, pocket-sized, wood panel that is an eighteenth century icon; the vintage Omega Constellation concealed in the depths of a job lot of second-hand watches from various hands. Admittedly, such finds have become rarer as the public becomes more educated by TV antiques programmes, but there is still a world of once-discarded things out there waiting to be discovered. All you have to do is look; yet how many times have you heard that member of the public on *Antiques Roadshow*, when his or her attention is drawn to a maker's mark, or a signature on a canvas, say, Oh, how interesting, I never noticed that before? Most people simply don't look at things, especially things they have owned for years. They are blinded by habituation.

I watch people. I listen in on them. Yesterday I was sitting outside Café Harlem with an espresso when two men in Hugo Boss suits and cheap shoes sat down a table away from me. They plonked their BlackBerries on the table, opened their briefcases, and took out some spreadsheets. Their talk was loud and I wasn't so much eavesdropping as overhearing. *The implications of the team costs should be borne by the financial model* ... I had just taken out my notebook and jotted down this sentence when I saw a blind man coming towards me, waving his long white wand from side to side like the antenna of a mine-detector. There was a faint metallic tick as it struck a bollard. I saw him adjust his step a fraction in response, and I reckoned he had just pinpointed his whereabouts. The bollard was a signpost, his whereabouts a sonic map, buzzing with echoic input. Ambient noise bouncing off surfaces, muffled by others. On the other hand, I surmised, he might not be blind at all, his accoutrements of cane and dark glasses a disguise. The Troubles might have ameliorated, but I guessed that no one really knew how much surveillance still went on. He negotiated his way through the opening of the sectioned-off pavement area. Tapping the legs of the aluminium furniture, he found the next table to me, sat down, and folded his cane. I took out a packet of American Spirit and rolled a cigarette. When I lit it with a vintage Dunhill lighter he tilted his head towards the rasp of the flint. Blind or not, he saw me in his own way. I got up and left. By now the businessmen were engrossed with their BlackBerries. All this time they had acted as if we did not exist.

When I hear the word BlackBerry I still think of the tangle of blackberry. Bramble. Berries that stain the hands and the lips. You won't find me on Facebook, and I don't do much email, though I find the internet useful for all kinds of research. I deal mainly by word of mouth and I like to meet my clients face to face, whether in public or private places. Besides the antiques, I deal in beneficial herbs, as Howard Marks calls them, though I'm no Howard Marks, with thirty-odd identities and paperwork to match; mine is a modest business, a private club that operates on personal recommendation. The herb is ethically and organically home-grown, on an intimate scale that puts it beyond the interests of the paramilitaries. I don't look like a dope-dealer. Yesterday I was wearing a navy-blue herringbone 1960s Burton suit with a white linen handkerchief stuffed in the breast pocket, white Oxford shirt with a sky blue stripe, brown knitted silk tie, oxblood Oxford shoes, and a grey fur-felt trilby. I am sixty-one. I'd taken to wearing handkerchiefs and hats a good few years ago, somewhat apprehensively at first, thinking my appearance would attract derision, especially from the young; but gradually I realised that the young have eyes only for themselves and that people my age are largely invisible. No one really sees that dapper gent, and I proceed through the city unmolested.

I'm trying to remember what I was wearing that evening outside the Morning Star when I last wrote in the missing notebook. It was October, and the Burton, cut from a heavy, pre-central-heating cloth, would have done well on that occasion. When I took it to Lazenbatt, the last tailor in Belfast, to be altered – it was an inch too big in the chest and waist – he remarked admiringly that the trousers could stand up on their own. But I hadn't yet bought the Burton suit. I cast my mind back and see myself at one of my wardrobes, selecting a burgundy knitted wool tie with a light blue Oxford shirt, navy and tan houndstooth Shetland wool jacket, grey flannels, and Crockett & Jones tan brogues. I stuffed a blue and yellow paisley silk handkerchief in my breast pocket, took a final look at myself in the cheval mirror, went downstairs, and strode out the door of 41 Elsinore Gardens. I'd be drinking later, so I took the bus into town.

As well as the Muji notebook and Waterman's pen, I was carrying the watch I had promised to show to my client, 1954 vintage, but in lovely condition, signed Longines and bearing the famous winged emblem. Ten-carat gold-filled rectangular case, about one and a half inches by one. Vintage watches are much smaller than modern ones, and people think they must be ladies' watches, but not so. This would have been worn by a man of some means. Dial with vertical stripe textured finish, raised gold-coloured cursive Arabic numerals at twelve, three, six and nine o'clock, the other hours marked by batons. Subsidiary seconds dial with cross-hairs, just above the six. Elegant gold lance-style hands. Original crystal, clean and clear. Snakeskin strap. I came across it in a zipped inner compartment of a ladies' 1950s snakeskin handbag on a stall at the Friday market, and was tempted to ask the dealer how much he wanted for the bag, and keep schtum about the watch; but I have my ethics, so I drew his attention to it. Well, well, he said, fancy that, I never thought to look inside. One of those old wind-up jobs, he said, let's say, twenty pounds? He looked hopeful. I knew he was doubling his estimate, so I made a face, offered him ten and we settled on fifteen. He thought he'd done well from the deal. Later I would offer it to my client for four hundred. He would say three, we'd settle on three-fifty, and the client would be well pleased. I'd paid Beringer, my watchmaker, sixty pounds to service it, so I'd made a tidy profit. But in truth my buyer would have made a good investment; not that he would ever sell it. So everyone was happy.

On the bus I took the watch from my pocket and checked the time against my own, another Longines, 1948, the year of my birth. Both read two minutes past three, and I was to meet my client at Muriel's bar at four.

2

RAPID EYE MOVEMENT

I replaced the Longines watch in my jacket pocket, took out my notebook, and read what I'd written the day before yesterday in the smoking area of Caffè Nero in Ann Street. I'd driven into town on one of my vintage clothes shopping expeditions. Ann Street has a couple of vintage shops, and there's another, Bang Vintage, round the corner in Church Lane where Muriel's is situated. Since the missing notebook remains missing, I cannot be certain as to what exactly I wrote in that notebook then, but I think it concerned an experience I sometimes have when I switch on the car radio and hear nothing beyond the ambient hum of the apparatus. I have it more or less permanently tuned to Radio 3 for the classical music, and know that the nothing signifies a lull between the movements of a piece, or the silence that follows the announcement of a piece, perhaps a live performance, and you can imagine the performer's hands poised over the keyboard of his instrument, about to approach the piece, readying himself for the onset – you can almost hear the expectant hush in the audience – or, if it is indeed that break between movements, and it is live, the silence might be betrayed by a muted fusillade of coughs, a rustling of chairs or shuffling of feet until there is complete silence, and then you hear the opening bars of the next movement emerging from the silence. At any rate, this is what I wrote the day before yesterday:

I'd just passed the Waterworks when I switched on the radio and got silence. Then the piece began, and as it proceeded I knew I was listening to Glenn Gould playing Bach's *Contrapunctus XIV* from *The Art of Fugue*. I pictured Gould, famously eccentric in his dress as in other aspects of his life, clothed in overcoat, muffler, hat and mittens even in midsummer, and then saw him hunched over the keyboard seated on the old chair his father had made for him, which he used even when the seat had completely worn through and his bottom was supported by nothing but the frame, swaying to the music, and as I listened to him playing I could hear the familiar background vocalizations, an almost coital groaning and crooning, ebbing and flowing and quavering with the dynamic of the music; his mother had told him to sing everything he played; he said his singing was unconscious, and increased proportionately with the inability of the piano in question to realize what he had in mind, the repeated or mirrored or inverted themes of *Contrapunctus XIV* intertwining, unfolding, recapitulating, as they had always done; and I wondered how many times I had heard this piece and where I was at the time, or what I was doing at the time, if anything, and as always I remembered the first time I had heard it, and who it was who introduced me to it, and where I was, and I wondered as I always did where he might be now, or what had become of him whether living or dead.

My CD of Gould's playing of *Contrapunctus XIV* lasts twelve minutes eighteen seconds, and I knew the piece had a good few

7

minutes to go when I got to the top deck of Castle Court car park. I let the engine run because if I switched it off I'd lose a few seconds of the performance. I knew how the piece ended, if that is the right word for a fugue which Bach never finished, and I see the video of Gould's playing *Contrapunctus XIV*, the camera close in to show the eyes behind the big square horn-rimmed glasses, the eyes sometimes open, half open or closed, the eyelids fluttering as if in REM sleep, dreaming the music, the mouth grimacing and smiling ecstatically, camera panning out to show all of Gould on the stage, until *Bang!* he punches out the final note before the shock of silence, a blank that strikes one almost bodily, and Gould throws up an arm as if shot, his index finger pointing to the heavens.

I turned off the engine. The radio stopped. I sat in the aftermath of the music for some minutes. I felt I had been somewhere else. In a state of fugue as it were, that temporary amnesia in which one loses the sense of oneself and takes on a life as another before coming to oneself again months or years later. Fugue, from Latin *fugere*, to flee.

When I got to Caffè Nero I wrote this all down, or what I remembered of it, knowing I'd written or thought of it many times before, thinking this time it might serve as a beginning or preamble to the book I had in mind, and again I try to picture the words I wrote in the missing notebook, but all I see is the rain-spattered page, all illegible splashes, blots and asterisks. And, as I write now in another notebook in 41 Elsinore Gardens, I try to see myself sitting outside the Morning Star, and I hear the rain drumming down on the awning and picture myself hunched over the missing notebook, cigarette in one hand, pen in the other, scribbling whatever words I wrote then. My eyes are wide open but it is as if I am dreaming. I am inside my mind floating outside myself looking down at myself, a disembodied mental eye or camera lens, I find I can pan round and see myself from different angles, and it is as if I see myself as someone else, the way that something I wrote years ago looks written by another; and in any event we never really see ourselves, all we see of ourselves is what we see in the mirror, ourselves reversed, which is not how others see us, we can never walk around ourselves and see what we look like from the back, so I float down and hover at my back and look over my shoulder at what I am writing, or what the other me was writing before the wind gusted a flurry of raindrops over the words, but try as I might the words swim and dissolve into splashes, blots and asterisks.

I pull myself away and see the other customer two tables away from me sitting before his pint. The brim of his trilby is pulled down so I can't see his face, but his body language looks familiar and I think maybe that is only because I have tried to picture him many times before, perhaps all I am remembering is a memory of a memory, or a speculation rather. In any event one could posit a relationship between these two figures brought together by whatever happenstance, a previous history in which they met each other in some other existence, that the man who was me, John Kilfeather, had met this man, let us call him Mr X, on some other occasion or several occasions, though I am pretty certain we had never met before. I suppose that at a certain point Mr X will come over to me and introduce himself to me as a stranger, and he will ask me what I am writing in my notebook, and I will not tell him the truth, for that would be too convoluted, and perhaps embarrassing, or seemingly pretentious, and in any event why should I tell him the truth, for the odds are that I and Mr X will never meet again, or perhaps we might, so I make up a story that will suit should we ever meet again. I could even give myself another name.

3

RUE DES BOUTIQUES OBSCURES

He was walking along Boulevard de Bonne Nouvelle in Paris, thinking of what had just happened to him in Rue du Sentier. It was cold and dark and foggy and the street lamps glowed dimly through the fog, their light shimmering in puddles on the street. He was wearing a double-breasted camel overcoat, red and white polka dot scarf, grey trilby, navy-blue corduroys, tan brogues and burgundy leather gloves. He was carrying a scuffed briefcase with the initials R.E.M. stamped on the flap above the brass lock. The initials were not his, as evidenced by the passport in his briefcase, which bore the name John Gabriel Kilpatrick and a photograph which did not look like him, taken four years previously. Also in the briefcase were a red, blue and green striped Kenzo scarf, three Muji A6 notebooks, a Muji A5 notebook, three Muji 0.5mm ink gel pens in black, blue and red, a map of Paris, an *Eyewitness Travel Guide* to Paris reprinted in 2005, and therefore five years out of date, a 1910 *Baedeker Paris*, and a novel by the contemporary French writer Patrick Modiano: John Kilpatrick was a travel writer and was in Paris for two weeks researching a book he intended to write about Paris which would feature extracts from books, fictional or otherwise, set in Paris, whether by writers living or dead. It was cold and he was glad of the burgundy leather gloves and he liked the feel of the hard leather briefcase handle in the soft leather grip of the glove and the feel of the cashmere lining on his hand within the glove. It was comforting to have that feeling after what had just happened to him in Rue du Sentier not ten minutes ago.

Earlier that day Kilpatrick had risen early in his hotel of choice, Hôtel Chopin in Passage Jouffroy off Boulevard Montmartre. The rooms were small but comfortable and the location was exceptional. Passage Jouffroy was one of the first such glass-roofed arcades in Paris, built in 1847, and contained an array of small retail outlets, among them Boutiques des Tuniques, selling blouses, shirts, robes, kimonos, scarves; Segas, walking-canes and theatrical antiques; Au Bonheur des Dames, embroidery; and Cinédoc, specializing in cinema books, posters and memorabilia. There was an entrance to the Musée Grevin, the waxworks museum on Boulevard Montmartre, though Kilpatrick had never ventured beyond its doors. Waxwork figures disturbed him.

After breakfast he went out for the day. It was a pleasant October morning, bright with a frosty nip in the air, and the soles of his brogues clacked musically on the hard pavement. He walked at random. Yesterday he had put in a good stint of research, visiting the Musée des Arts et Métiers and writing detailed descriptions of some of the architectural models on display, miniature simulacra of actual buildings in Paris, wonderful in the precision of their construction. He felt he deserved a break. Towards midday he found himself on the Rive Gauche in Le Bon Marché department store, designed by Gustave Eiffel and opened in 1852. It was warm indoors and he took off his red, blue and green striped Kenzo scarf and put it into the briefcase he was carrying. As he did so he thought this was an opportunity to buy a new scarf. He liked to buy at least one item of clothing in any location he might be visiting, items which would serve as souvenirs or aides-memoire, tangible connections with the past, redolent with association. The Rome shirt, the Berlin hat, the New York wingtip shoes which every time he put them on reminded him of the manhole covers of New York, massive antique cast-iron shields embossed with their makers' names, Abbott Hardware Company Ironworks, Marcy Foundry, Etna Iron Works, Madison Ironworks, Cornell's Iron Works, the words making themselves felt underfoot when he walked on them.

He proceeded to Soldes Mode Hommes and after a perusal of the neckwear department chose a heavy silk red and white polka dot scarf with a cashmere backing. He had just left the store when he thought of the other scarf he might have bought instead, a blue and gold paisley that might have gone better with the camel coat, though it cost somewhat more. He put the thought behind him. He put on the red and white polka dot scarf.

That afternoon, at Librairie Jean Tuzot on Rue Saint Sulpice, Kilpatrick bought a book by Patrick Modiano, *Rue des boutiques obscures*, and leafed through it before buying it, as he knew he would. He had first come across Modiano some time ago and had since bought four of his books from online French booksellers. Though they all seemed to be versions of each other, he was attracted by their fugue-like repetition of themes and imagery, their evocation of a noir Paris in which the protagonists were endlessly in search of their identities. He put the book in his briefcase.

Towards nightfall he was walking vaguely in the direction of the hotel, up Rue du Sentier in the garment district, when the thought of the scarf came to him again, and he pictured himself wearing the paisley silk, seeing it gleam against the soft wool and cashmere of the camel coat. By now it was cold and dark and foggy and the street lamps glowed dimly through the fog, their light shimmering in puddles on the street, and as he pictured himself in the scarf he saw a man walking down the other side of Rue du Sentier. The man was wearing a double-breasted camel overcoat, blue and gold paisley scarf, grey trilby, navy-blue corduroys, tan brogues and burgundy leather gloves. He was carrying a briefcase.

The man in question stopped at a shop window under a streetlamp as if window-shopping. Kilpatrick stopped too. The man turned and looked at Kilpatrick. His face was half-hidden by the brim of his hat. Then, with the gesture of a magician who has come to the end of his stage act, he swept off the hat, made a low bow, and vanished into the darkness beyond the oasis of lamplight. Kilpatrick walked over to the window. There was no-one there. The glass was dusty and the only item on display was a mannequin dressed in the fashion of the Sixties – slim-cut Prince of Wales windowpane check suit, tab-collar shirt and narrow knitted tie, a snap-brim trilby at a tipsy angle on its head. Its arms were thrown out and one leg had buckled under it. It was the kind of shape one might cut in a sixties dance, thought Kilpatrick. The Frug or some such. Several dead flies lay at the mannequin's feet and Kilpatrick wondered who had last set foot in the place. He looked at the impassive features of the mannequin, and thought of the face he had just seen. Kilpatrick thought of the face of his erstwhile friend John Bourne, who had vanished some years ago, and had not been seen since by anyone of Kilpatrick's acquaintance. Kilpatrick entered the shop doorway and tried the handle of the door. The door was locked.

4

OPIUM

———◆◆◆———

As I write, I have notebooks strewn on the desk, on the sofa, on the floor, and I refer to them from time to time, or rather I flit from one to another, skimming, flicking through the pages from back cover to front and back again, foraging for I know not what, a glimmer of a memory, a phrase, a string of words, something jotted down a week, a month, a year ago, that might be germane to this present moment, something that is in my mind or on my mind now as it was then. One of the problems with the notebooks is their fundamental lack of organisation. Some are dated on the cover, others bear a title which might indicate their contents or preoccupations, some are both titled and dated, and some individual items are dated, but many are not. Consequently, although the cover of a notebook might be dated, there is no guarantee that a particular passage will have been written around that time, for in practice I sometimes pick up any notebook that is at hand rather than the current one.

Some entries are neatly written, some are scribbled, some are so scrawled as to be illegible, so that the writing seems the product of several hands, written by different people. Some entries are quotations from other writers, though many have no quotation marks, and sometimes I am uncertain as to whether a particular entry is my own work, or the work of another, or an amalgam of the two. Whatever the case, I like to think of that other work as being written by myself. Indeed, some of the notebooks carry my name, John Kilfeather, on the inside cover, and my address, as a form of security. A proof of my identity. Then again some entries which must have made sense to me at the time of writing make little or no sense to me now. You might say that I am faced with a jigsaw puzzle. But this is not a jigsaw puzzle. There are no straight edges or corners to help with the framing of the picture; and the picture or the story I am trying to piece together does not yet exist.

I open a notebook at random, and come across this: 'Dublin train 11.00/13.20 JULES VERNE Cocteau 80 days'. The cover of the notebook is dated Dec. 2009, and I now remember what I had forgotten, that I first read Jean Cocteau's *Round the World Again in 80 Days (Mon Premier Voyage)* on the Belfast–Dublin Enterprise Express. 11.00/13.20 must refer to the train times, though I cannot remember which train I took, or on what day, or why I made the journey, for the entry is undated. Cocteau was inspired by a stage production, at the Châtelet Theatre, of Jules Verne's novel, as indicated on the first page of Cocteau's book. 'Never for me,' writes Cocteau, 'will any real ocean have the glamour of that sheet of green canvas, heaved on the back of the Châtelet stage-hands crawling like caterpillars beneath it, while Phileas and Passepartout from the dismantled hull watch the lights of Liverpool twinkling in the distance.'

In 1936, at the suggestion of his then lover Marcel Khill, Cocteau undertook to duplicate Verne's adventure, securing financial backing from the evening paper *Paris-Soir*, to whom he would send a series of instalments along the way. He soon discovered that Phileas Fogg's journey in 1873 was indeed a fiction, and that even in 1936 it was barely possible. The practical arrangements were made by Khill, whose real name was Mustapha Marcel Khelilou ben Abdelkader, born of an Algerian father and a Norman mother. Throughout Cocteau's account Khill is referred to as Passepartout, the French for a master key, skeleton key, or picture mount, rather than passport. Khill was also Cocteau's opium supplier, and one of the features of the book is their constant and frequently rewarded search for opium dens. Much of the book reads like an opium dream.

My notebook contains five pages of notes with page references to Cocteau's book written with a Muji 0.5mm black ink gel pen written at my table seat on the Enterprise Express. They are followed by a pencilled entry, most likely written at a later date: 'cf. Notebooks of Robert Frost, p. 89, Every thing that is a thing is out there and there it stands waiting under your eye till some day you notice it, p. 127, The strangeness is all in thinking two things at once, in being in two places at once. That is all there is to metaphor.' And when I read Cocteau's book I was indeed in two places at once. I do not know how many times I have been on the Dublin train, but the journey is so familiar to me that were I blindfolded I would have a good idea of where I was at whatever time, at whichever point on the line. Lisburn – Portadown – Newry – Dundalk – Drogheda – Dublin. I might well have been in Lisburn, a nondescript market town, I might have glanced out the window at a row of backyards – washing lines, pigeon lofts, sheds – before writing, '8, I owe much to the Rome express'. I stretch my hand up to the bookshelf on the wall above my desk in 41 Elsinore Gardens and take down Cocteau's book, which has languished there unopened for I do not know how long, open it at page 8, and begin to read these words I now transcribe:

'I owe much to the Rome express. It cleared my mind of cobwebs, the befuddlement of one who after many years of sleep is woken with a start; it resolved the difficulty I had found in living on my own resources instead of suffering the lot of a somnambulist walking precariously along the edges of a roof ... Now at last I was submerged – how marvellous it was! – in simple, human sleep, dense and opaque, broken by lucid intervals when I rose to the surface and saw between my feet the landscape scudding past, framed in the carriage window. Trains play Beethoven symphonies. Memories of their themes float up, and automatically blend into the breathless rhythms of speed. It is as if the deafness from which they sprang were akin to the silence of the railway carriage, a complex silence made up of innumerable noises. The throbbing pulse of blood through its dark metronome of arteries, echoes of triumphal marches, glimpses of nightbound stations and, by day, of white, almost Moorish cities, with minarets, square-built houses and lines of fluttering linen hung along the foreshore of a sea dyed laundry-blue – all compose the intervals of a dream theatre where dramas inexpressible in words are played.'

I came to the end of Cocteau's *Round the World Again in 80 Days* as the Enterprise Express pulled into Connolly Station in Dublin.

I know this because the last note in my sequence reads, 'Read in 2 hrs 15 mins – pulling into Dublin.' I had been in another world. The translation I read is by Stuart Gilbert and appeared in 1937. Gilbert also translated Georges Simenon and Jean-Paul Sartre, and assisted in the French translation of James Joyce's *Ulysses*. As I write these words it occurs to me that I should read Cocteau in Cocteau's French. I order the book online from the cryptically named Tgl Harmattan 2, Paris, France, thinking of myself in Paris, thinking of Joyce blinding in Paris, naming, for his party-piece, the shops along O'Connell Street.

5

PILOT LIGHT

It was night. He was walking along Boulevard de Bonne Nouvelle in Paris when he glanced up and saw the blue and white enamel sign that read Boulevard de Bonne Nouvelle. I've taken a wrong turn, he thought, and doubled back along the boulevard in the direction of Hôtel Chopin, walking until it became Boulevard de la Poissonière, which in turn became Boulevard Montmartre, the same line of boulevard under different names. He walked until he came to Passage Jouffroy. It was night and the iron gate was locked. He pressed the intercom button under the words Hôtel Chopin. He heard a hiss as if of static. Kilpatrick, he said. He heard the gate click and he pictured the night porter at reception. He opened the gate and stepped over its threshold and the gate clanged shut behind him, echoing in the empty arcade. The closed shops were dimly lit from within. Night light. What was the word? *Veilleuse.* He walked past a window in which stood a headless mannequin wearing a dressing-gown of blue and gold silk brocade and he thought again of the blue and gold paisley scarf he had not bought in Bon Marché knotted round the neck of a male bust, its generic face blank under the grey trilby. He fingered the red and white polka dot scarf at his throat and thought of the man he had seen in Rue du Sentier. It seemed long ago.

He pushed open the hotel entrance door and entered the foyer. There was no one at reception, but his key was there on the desk, attached to a heavy wooden tab which bore the number 36. He mounted the three steps to the lift and pressed button 3. He waited. There was no response. He pressed again but still nothing. He turned to the dark staircase and depressed the timer light switch. What was the word? *Minuterie.* He remembered it was also the word for the timer in an explosive device. As he came to the first floor the light went out and he had a brief phantom image of the lighted staircase. He groped his way to the landing and pressed the next timer switch, hurrying his footsteps so as to remain in the light. On the third floor he unlocked the door to Room 36. He went in. He switched on the light. He put his briefcase on the floor. He took off his hat, scarf and overcoat and laid them on the bed. He took off the tweed jacket he had been wearing under the overcoat and laid the jacket on the bed. He went into the bathroom, went to the washstand, loosened his tie, rolled up his sleeves, turned on the tap and splashed water on his face. Blind for a few seconds, he groped for the towel on the rail beside the washstand. He dried his face and his hands. When he replaced the towel on the rail he saw that the wall to the right of the rail was splashed with water that must have dripped from his hands as he moved from the washstand and groped for the towel, and he remembered that a similar pattern had occurred every time he had splashed water on his face, whether after shaving first thing in the morning or splashing water on his face last thing at night, and he remembered that afterwards

22

he did not remember it until the next time it happened, and then it reminded him of all the other times.

The splashes had dribbled in rivulets on the wall and he remembered thinking on those other occasions what he was thinking now, that they were like a river delta or a root system or a route map: if in the morning, an augury of the path he would take that day; if at night, a portent of what he would dream. He looked into the mirror and for a brief instant it seemed the mirror was a dark portal into Rue du Sentier where the man had appeared from and then vanished into the dark. He saw the street like a stage set and the man like a magician taking his bow to the audience that was Kilpatrick, except Kilpatrick could not see himself, all he saw was the man dressed in the clothes Kilpatrick had been dressed in. He came to and saw himself looking back at himself and he wondered how many hundreds of faces had appeared in the mirror before his, the many who had looked in the mirror and how many were living or dead. He wondered if the mirror had a memory of those faces or for those faces. He thought that for all he knew the man in question might have looked into this mirror too.

He went back into the room and hung up the clothes that had been lying on the bed. He turned on the bedside lamp and turned off the ceiling light and lay down on the bed in the clothes he was wearing. The lamp had a dimmer switch and he turned it to its lowest setting. *Veilleuse.* Night light, sidelight, pilot light. *Mettre en veilleuse*, to dim, to put on the back burner. From *veille*, a period of wakefulness; *la veille*, the day before yesterday. *La veille de sa mort*, the eve of his death. *Homme de veille*, night watchman.

In the dim light of the bedside lamp he closed his eyes and thought of himself watching himself or watching over himself. He fell asleep.

He was in the Crown Bar in Belfast. The dream was in the present but it was set back in time because the bar was lit by dim strip lighting and not the original gas lighting that had been reinstalled when they restored the bar after the bombings of the seventies and the eighties. Kilpatrick was standing at the marble-topped counter. There were three other men at the counter beside him, separated by their own space, all of them gazing at the display of bottles ranged on shelves before the mirrors of the reredos or gazing at their reflections in the mirrors. The man to his right turned quizzically towards him and said, Nice jacket. The man was wearing a tan three-button hacking jacket buttoned at the middle button. Nice jacket yourself, said Kilpatrick, and the man smiled. What's that you're drinking? John Powers? he said, and he gestured to the barman. Same again, he said, pointing to Kilpatrick's drink and his own.

John Bourne, he said, extending his hand. Kilpatrick shook the hand and said, John Kilpatrick. Two Johns, said John Bourne, I think you should be Kilpatrick, and I'll be Bourne. Saves confusion, don't you think? Nice Donegal tweed, said Bourne, where did you get it? Oh, you know, the Friday market, said Kilpatrick, Yours? It's my father's, said Bourne, he died in it. He pointed to a frayed hole in the breast pocket. Couldn't bear to get rid of it, Savile Row. The old man had taste. Of course, odds are, yours is a dead man's jacket too, except you don't know who he was, though for all you know you might have crossed him in

24

the street years ago, before he died, and you thought, nice jacket, not knowing you'd end up wearing it some day. It's a good fit, said Bourne. Think it was made for you.

The barman put two John Powers on the counter. John Bourne raised his glass and John Kilpatrick raised his glass. They were about to clink when the strip lighting began to flicker and Kilpatrick remembered that the Crown was due another bombing and he woke up as he always did before the bomb went off. For a moment he did not know where he was. Then he remembered he was where he had been, lying in the clothes he had been wearing before he fell asleep in the dim light of Room 36, Hôtel Chopin, Paris.

6

THE VANISHING COIN

Today I gave the Livingstone suit its first outing. I'd bought it on eBay and it arrived neatly parcelled two days ago, a beautiful chestnut brown herringbone with a faint orange windowpane check, jacket with slanted hacking pockets, working cuffs, high-rise narrow-cut trousers with turn-ups. The seller, Bookman17, knowing that a good picture is worth a thousand words, had provided a comprehensive photographic gallery of the item displayed on a tailor's dummy. There were close-ups of the weave. I was mesmerized. I made it an item on My eBay Watch list, and returned to it and watched it for a good few minutes every day of the seven-day auction, imagining myself clothed in it and how it would feel on. I was the only bidder. The measurements given in the description accorded to mine, and when I tried on the suit it was nearly a perfect fit. A bit neat in the body of the jacket, but the sleeve length perfect, ending at the wrist bone, the trouser bottom resting nicely as it should on the shoe. When I looked, I discovered, sewn into the inside jacket pocket, a handwritten tailor's label which read *Major R.E. Livingstone 9/10/66*, on which day I was eighteen, so I could as easily call it the birthday suit.

The Livingstone suit forced me to adopt a somewhat military

posture, but that would relax with time as I wore it in. I could see it being worn by a character in my book, one John Harland, who had vanished without trace some ten years ago. And in wearing the suit, as with other items of vintage clothing I had purchased over the years, I would think myself into the character of Harland: a kind of method writing, not unlike method acting, where the actor – think Brando, Newman, Pacino – immerses himself in the part by drawing on his own emotions, discovering, through affective memory, those experiences in his own life which correspond to the fictional experiences of the character he is to portray, and reliving his own experiences onstage or onscreen as the 'character'. He lives in a parallel world. Think De Niro in *Taxi Driver* looking into a mirror at himself, saying, 'You talkin' to me? You talkin' to me? You talkin' to *me*?'

I took another look at myself, John Kilfeather, in the mirror. The russet brown and orange of the tweed glowed like autumn leaves in the autumn sunlight that flooded in through the bay window, the cloth seeming to undulate and vibrate as I moved this way and that, and not for the first time I wished I could see myself in the round, as another might see me, or as I might were I to stand outside myself. I felt high. I undid the cuff buttons of one sleeve and rolled it back in the manner of Jean Cocteau, imagining my hand emerging from the sleeves as his hand, that elegant long-fingered hand theatrically yet nonchalantly posed, and it was not difficult to imagine myself floating through my 1930s cheval mirror – how many faces has it seen? – to see or be the Jean Cocteau whose *Orphée* appeared in 1950, Orpheus who travels to the Underworld through a mirror, Orpheus who ignores his wife to listen for messages on the car radio in the car parked in the under-floor-level garage, enigmatic phrases travelling through the static of the Underworld. Never music, always words. *L'oiseau chante avec ses doigts. Deux fois …*

As it is, I am walking through Belfast in the Livingstone suit, the birthday suit. I feel all yin and yang, both rough and smooth as the October sun flickers on some surfaces and glows on others and the suit ripples to a sympathetic rhythm as it moves and I move with it as if it were a second skin. I stroll down Royal Avenue and barely a soul gives me a glance, let alone a second glance, for barely a soul sees me. I am not on their radar. But you can be sure that if *I* saw someone wearing such a suit, you can be sure *I* would notice, but then everyone is not me, nor I them. I am a ghost. Barely a soul takes me under their notice, only the one I hear playing the fiddle from afar, who cannot yet see me, nor I him, but I know his music of old, I know that dance I heard last week, and heard the week before, but this time it is different, as it was before, yet will be as it always was, the melody that haunts itself in its own ever-changing repetitions, intertwining, unfolding, recapitulating, speaking of Transylvania in the loops and spirals of the melody, lingering for all its quickness, the bow leaning into and off the notes in little elegant embellishments more audible with every step I take or dance, I picture his long-fingered left hand seeming barely to move, the bow hand minimal in its movement, and I wonder again how he does it, and I walk towards the source, knowing he has seen me coming through the crowd, timing the tune to end as I am about to drop a coin in his cup and take off my hat to him, whereupon with some aplomb he synchronizes the doffing of his hat with mine and I say, Nice music as always, and he will

28

say, Thank you, sir. We both know a good hat when we see one. Other than that I glide through the crowds unacknowledged, haunting the same streets and alleyways I have been walking for how many weeks I do not know.

I was in town to see Beringer the watchmaker, and as I walked I thought of when I had last been in his workshop. I had climbed into the whispering, ticking attic and had taken in the various faces of the clocks – carriage clocks, mantel clocks, clocks under glass domes, clocks supported by Grecian columns, clocks with dials of ceramic and enamel – and had remarked on how well he had them synchronized, or so it seemed to me. Yes, but if you listen, said Beringer, they all tick out slightly of synch, if only in a manner of speaking, and if you look at the relative positions of the second hands, you'll see they're all out of synch too, and even if any two were in synch, why, that would just be coincidence, because real time is fuzzy time, strictly speaking it's not the same time in any other corner of the attic as it is in this, since time is a function of space, if you believe Einstein, so strictly speaking we all live in different time zones, since our bodies occupy different spaces. Timewise we live in a serial fuzz. He giggled.

We talked a little of the Roma fiddler, whose playing I knew Beringer knew. I remarked on the magic of his playing, and Beringer said, You want to see magic, you want to see magic? He took a coin from his pocket, displayed it theatrically for my perusal, then balanced it on two fingertips of his left hand, clicked the fingers of his right hand, and it vanished. One second it was there, one incalculably tiny fraction of a second later it was not.

That's brilliant, I said, I didn't know you could do magic, how did you do it? That would be telling, he said, but he showed me anyway. You know the thing about magic, he said, it's like when you lose something you know was at hand a few minutes ago, say a pen, and when you look for it, it's not there, you turn the place upside down for it, you retrace your movements in your memory, you look everywhere there is to look but it's not there, it's as if you'd slipped into another dimension identical to this one, a parallel world, but with one tiny, crucial difference – the pen does not exist in the other world you've found yourself in. And I thought of the missing notebook.

7

PASSAGE DES PANORAMAS

———◆·◆·◆———

He went back to sleep. He dreamed he had got out of bed and drawn the curtains of the mansard window. He looked out. The fog had gone and a full moon shone in the sky. He looked down on the rooftops of Paris which in the moonlight were purple and velvety and edged along with ridges and chimneys of chalk white. He stood there for a long while before going back to bed. When he woke in the morning it was broad daylight and the sun streamed in through the mansard window. As he shaved himself before the mirror Kilpatrick looked at himself and thought, as he had often thought before, how in a foreign country one could be anyone, and that indeed we are all close to the brink of being someone else.

The day before yesterday, on a whim, he had gone into an 'Irish' bar called the James Joyce. He stood at the bar counter and ordered a John Jameson's and had taken a sip when a red-faced man at the other end of the bar came over to him and said, Nice coat. The man's accent was educated English. He was ever so slightly drunk. He was carrying a black briefcase. Nice coat yourself, said Kilpatrick. The man's coat was standard Hugo Boss issue and at least one size too big for him. Haven't I seen you somewhere before? said the red-faced man, I swear I saw you on Boulevard Raspail the other day. Kilpatrick did not think he had set foot on Boulevard Raspail since he arrived in Paris, and said so. Well, said the man dubiously, then it was a look-alike, same hat, same coat, same scarf. He looked down at Kilpatrick's feet. Same briefcase, he said, funny old world, isn't it? The man extended his hand. Freddy Gabriel, he said, British Council. John Kilmore, said Kilpatrick, on a sudden whim, and they shook hands. They talked, and Kilpatrick told Gabriel he was in Paris looking at shirting fabrics, he was setting up a bespoke shirt business in Dublin. He found himself talking knowledgeably about collars, plackets, cuffs, the provenance of linens and cottons. He almost believed himself.

In the morning Kilpatrick took the lift down. Unlike the night before, it had come when summoned. He was about to go into the breakfast room when the concierge came over to him. Mr Kilpatrick? A letter for you. She extended an envelope. Kilpatrick was puzzled. So far as he knew, no-one knew he was in Paris, let alone in Hôtel Chopin. He looked at the envelope. Expensive, thick wove paper. It bore the words, *By Hand*, underlined twice, and his name, *John Kilpatrick*, written with fountain pen in an elegant italic hand that was unfamiliar to him. He opened the envelope. A sheet of matching notepaper, an old-style French latchkey. Dear John, he read, If you go to 41 Rue du Sentier Thursday night at seven o'clock you will find something to your advantage. Trust me. Enclosed find the key. From one John to another, I am, yours truly, John. Kilpatrick went over to the concierge and enquired if she had seen the bearer of the letter. No, it was in Monsieur's pigeonhole – *le casier* – when she took over from the night porter that morning. Kilpatrick put the envelope with its contents into his briefcase. Over breakfast he looked at the letter, turning the key in his hand, pondering its import. It was Tuesday. He decided to put the affair on the back burner, what was the expression? *Mettre en veilluese.*

He would begin that morning with a stroll through Passage des Panoramas, whose entrance lay immediately opposite Passage Jouffroy, on the other side of Boulevard Montmartre. He planned to write an extensive piece on the Paris arcades, quoting extracts from Walter Benjamin's *The Arcades Project.* Kilpatrick had transcribed some of these into an A5 notebook. Benjamin's *The Arcades Project* was itself one huge notebook, transcribed from many notebooks, originally organised by topic into sheaves or 'convolutes', with passages sometimes repeated, sometimes redrafted or revised in only marginally different forms, interspersed with citations from an array of nineteenth century authors, but also from the work of key contemporaries – Marcel Proust, Paul Valéry, André Breton, Ernst Bloch, Theodor Adorno, among others, until citation eventually outnumbered Benjamin's own commentaries, and the distinction between Benjamin's words and the words of others became more and more blurred, voices refracted through the medium of Benjamin's mind. He saw Paris as the capital of the nineteenth century. His book was a dream representation of Paris itself, images and phrases intertwining in a vast fugal architecture, echoing rooms and galleries of language. Kilpatrick opened his notebook at random and read:

'One knew of places in ancient Greece where the way led down into the underworld. Our waking existence is like a land which, at certain hidden points, leads down into the underworld – a land full of inconspicuous places from which dreams arise. All day long, suspecting nothing, we pass them by, but no sooner has sleep come than we eagerly grope our way back to lose ourselves in the dark corridors. By day, the labyrinth of urban dwellings resembles consciousness; the arcades, which are galleries leading into the city's past, issue unacknowledged onto the streets. At night, however, under the tenebrous mass of the houses, their more compacted darkness bursts forth like a threat, and the nocturnal pedestrian hurries past – unless we have emboldened him to turn into the narrow alley.'

Another entry, headed 'Blanqui': 'There exists a world where a man follows the road that, in the other world, his double did not take. His existence divides in two, a globe for each; it bifurcates a second time, a third time, thousands of times. He thus possesses fully formed doubles with innumerable variants, which, in multiplying, always represent him as a person but capture only fragments of his destiny. All that one might have been in this world, one is in another. Along with one's entire existence from birth to death, experienced in a multitude of places, one also lives, in yet other places, ten thousand different versions of it ... The number of our doubles is infinite in time and space. These doubles exist in bone and flesh – indeed, in trousers and jacket, crinoline and chignon. They are by no means phantoms; they are the present eternalized.'

As he emerged from Passage Jouffroy into Boulevard Montmartre, Kilpatrick considered the fact that this sunlit Paris was not all there was to Paris. Beneath his feet lay a subterranean otherworld of stairways, hallways, portals, tunnels, quarries, pillars, archways, bunkers, cellars, dungeons, roadways, wells, mines, caves, chambers, caverns, crypts, catacombs, vaults, grottoes, galleries of human bones, dead city layered upon dead city, infiltrated by the living. He was walking over an invisible abyss. He crossed the boulevard and entered the portal of Passage des Panoramas.

8

ATOMS AND STARS

———◆·◆·◆———

Good trick, Bill, I said. Magic. Always a pleasure to do business, Ben, said Beringer. These were not our real names. He was John Beringer, I was John Kilfeather. We used to call each other John until one night after a smoke of Red Leb – how many years ago was that, Red Leb? – he came out with, Flobbalob, Little Weed. The *Flower Pot Men*. We spent a good hour trying to remember the children's TV series of the 1950s and 60s. I've just looked it up online, and I here transcribe the Wikipedia entry:

'Originally, the programme was part of a BBC children's television series titled *Watch with Mother*, with a different programme each weekday, and all involving string puppets. The *Flower Pot Men* was the story of two little men made of flower pots who lived at the bottom of an English suburban garden. The plot changed little in each episode. The programme always took place in a garden, behind a potting shed. The third character was Little Weed, of indeterminate species, resembling a sunflower or dandelion with a smiling face, growing between two large flowerpots. The three were also sometimes visited by a tortoise called Slowcoach. While "the man who worked in the garden" was away having his dinner the two Flower Pot Men, Bill and Ben, emerged from the two flowerpots. After a minor adventure a minor mishap occurs; someone is guilty. "Which of those two flower pot men, was it Bill or was it Ben?" the narrator trills, in a quavering soprano; the villain confesses; the gardener's footsteps are heard coming up the garden path; the Flower Pot Men vanish into their pots and the closing credits roll. The final punch-line was, "And I think the little house knew something about it! Don't *you*?" '

As I researched Bill and Ben I looked up another children's TV series of the early 70s, *Mr Benn*. In each episode Mr Benn, wearing a black suit and bowler hat, leaves his house at 52 Festive Road and visits a fancy-dress costume shop where he is invited by the moustachioed, fez-wearing shopkeeper to try on a particular outfit. He leaves the shop through a magic door at the back of the changing room and enters a world appropriate to his costume. The series also appeared in book form, and I quote from one: 'Mr Benn changed into the space outfit in no time. He looked at himself in the mirror and then headed for the door that always led to adventures. On the other side he found himself in a spaceship.' Towards the end of the narrative, as always, the shopkeeper reappears to lead him back to the changing room, and the story ends. Mr Benn returns to his normal life, but is left with a small souvenir, proof of his magical adventure. I pictured myself in the changing room, looking at myself in the mirror dressed as an Arabian prince, about to embark on the *Magic Carpet* adventure.

As for the Flower Pot Men, they spoke a mangled idiolect which sounded like English but not quite. *Flobbalob Bill. Flobbadob Ben.* After the Red Leb episode, we referred to each other as Bill and Ben. Some people called us Bee and Kay, others, John and John, the two Johns. Red Leb, must have been around 1974, said Beringer, I think I remember someone gave me a blast of Red Leb after the Smithfield fire-bombing, and we began on one of our reminiscences of the vanished Smithfield Market and its glassed-over arcades, its nave and transepts crossed by narrow passages lined with sagging bookshelves, old furniture and bric-a-brac. It was in Smithfield that I first came across Cathal O'Byrne's book about Belfast, *As I Roved Out*, and the Smithfield of my dreams would be haunted by his, a veritable rookery of hallways, alleyways and gangways, leading up to balconies – each with its nest of dwelling places – higher and ever higher. I glide through Smithfield like a revenant from the future. At a bookstall I look over the shoulder of the young man who stands immersed in a book, the reader who was me.

It's like another world, says Beringer. For all we know it exists in another world where Smithfield didn't get firebombed. As do we, only different, I suppose, you know, Many Worlds theory. Quantum incoherence, don't expect me to give you the maths of it, but in layman's terms, I mean our terms, it means reality is like a tree with an infinite number of branches, an infinite number of outcomes. Many Worlds accounts for that, as many worlds as there are possibilities. Didn't you have something in that book you were writing, what was it called, *XYZ*, what ever happened to that?

He was right. One of the sources quoted or paraphrased in my abandoned book, *X+Y=K*, was the Irish experimental physicist Fournier d'Albe, who in his book, *Two New Worlds*, published in 1908, proposed a hierarchical clustering model for the structure of the universe which anticipated modern fractal theory. Fournier's fractal was a snowflake pattern consisting of five parts; each of those parts was a miniature copy of that snowflake; those miniature copies were composed of still smaller snowflakes, and so on, in a dizzying blizzard of self-replication. Worlds lay within worlds in nested frequencies. Atoms and stars, electrons and planets, cells and galaxies all moved to the same measure. Clouds, earthquakes, river deltas, root systems, coastlines, music, fluid turbulence, the fluctuations of the stock market: all corresponded. A flag snaps back and forth in the wind, and a column of cigar smoke breaks into an anxious swirl. A pirouette of litter on a street corner heralds a tornado. A pin drops in an auditorium, a bomb goes off. Like patterns were apparent everywhere. The All was immutable, but the detail was ever new. The event, the incident, the individual was unique, unprecedented, irrecoverable; but the equilibrium was eternal, and death could have no dominion over the infinity of worlds.

Given these wide parameters, Fournier d'Albe thought it reasonable to assume that one could find a portal to that infinity of worlds, or at least to a parallel world. He immersed himself in the study of paranormal phenomena, including the mediumistic seances of the time. Of particular interest to me was the fact that in 1921 he investigated a spiritualist group in Belfast known as the Goligher Circle, centred around the sixteen-year-old medium Kathleen Goligher, who claimed to be in contact with a spirit world, the Other Side. Seances were conducted in the attic of their own home. Fournier d'Albe was curious to see if the phenomena that appeared to occur there could be replicated at a neutral location, and to that purpose he rented an unfurnished attic at 14 Exchange Place, a narrow lane – an entry, in Belfast parlance – off Lower North Street. After subjecting Kathleen Goligher to a series of rigorous controls he concluded that the 'paranormal phenomena' produced by her in collaboration with the Circle were nothing more than cheap conjuring tricks. Of further interest to me was the fact that John Harland had rented an attic at 14 Exchange Place for some months prior to his disappearance in the year 2001.

9

BLANK WHO

———————◆◆◆———————

In Passage des Panoramas Kilpatrick stopped and ordered a coffee at a table outside Gocce di Caffè. The Drop of Coffee. From his briefcase he took out *Rue des boutiques obscures*, the Patrick Modiano novel he had bought in St Sulpice. Published by Gallimard, 1978. Gallimard also published the complete works of Jean Cocteau, he remembered. He read the blurb on the back cover of *Rue des boutiques obscures*.

Qui pousse un certain Guy Roland, employé d'une agence de police privée que dirige un baron balte, à partir à la recherche d'un inconnu, disparu depuis longtemps? Le besoin de se retrouver lui-même après des années d'amnesie? Au cours de sa recherche, il receuille des bribes de la vie de cet homme qui était peut-être lui et à qui, de toute façon, il finit par s'identifier: What impels a certain Guy Roland, employee of a private detective agency overseen by a Baltic baron, to leave in search of an unknown man, long since disappeared? The need to find himself again after years of amnesia? In the course of his search, he recollects fragments of the life of this man who is perhaps himself, and who, in any case, he ends up identifying with.

He turned to the beginning of *Rue des boutiques obscures* and read the opening sentences: *Je ne suis rien. Rien qu'une silhouette claire, ce soir-là, à la terrace d'un café.* I am nothing. Nothing but a clear silhouette, this evening, on a café terrace. He wondered about his translation for the word *claire*. It was one of those words that might mean a number of things in English, and 'clear silhouette' did not sound like something one would say in English. Clear-cut? Clean? Sharp? Transparent? Limpid? These, too, did not seem quite right. And should *silhouette* be 'outline'? Kilpatrick thought he knew what the expression meant in French, he could see the man in question in his mind's eye, but somehow he could not find the proper English words. It was as if a fog intervened between one language and the other, the person who was thinking in one language lost to the one who thought in the other. His coffee arrived and he put the book away, thinking of himself as the unknown man sitting outside a café in Passage des Panoramas, a blank silhouette. Unknown, certainly, to those who passed him by, tourists, casual strollers, browsers, shoppers, others whose purposeful stride suggested native Parisians, for whom the *passage* was a short-cut, a matter of daily routine. Perhaps he was known in a manner of speaking to the man who had served him his coffee, for Kilpatrick had taken coffee there before, and the same man had served him then; but then he doubted if the man remembered him from among the hundreds of customers he must have served since then, and though he had nodded to Kilpatrick as he set his coffee on the table – *Voilà, un café, monsieur* – he did not think it was a nod of recognition. He finished his coffee and continued down Passage des Panoramas.

He stopped at a stamp shop called La Postale, one of several in the arcade, traditionally a philatelists' haven. French stamps, naturally. As a boy Kilpatrick had collected stamps, specializing in those of Ireland and the British Empire, and only gradually realizing that France had had an empire nearly as extensive as that of Britain. His eye was caught by two stamps on a display card headed 1948, one commemorating Louis Braille, the other Louis Auguste Blanqui, bearing portraits of their subjects. Kilpatrick knew Blanqui from his reading of Walter Benjamin, Blanqui the revolutionary who during one of his many terms of imprisonment had written *L'Eternité par les astres*, in which he propounded a universe of infinite worlds and endlessly repeated variations, endlessly doubled lives. Kilpatrick had toyed with the idea that Blanqui could be translated as Blank Who. As for Braille, when he thought of Braille he thought of Louis Braille as a boy stumbling in his father's saddler's shop, clutching the stitching-awl that an instant later would blind him, and of Braille punching out the raised dots of his writing system with the selfsame awl. Braille sounded like an awl. *Une braille.*

At that instant he remembered the blind man he would often see crossing his path in Belfast, waving his long white wand from side to side like the antenna of a mine-detector, the cane ticking against street furniture: lamp-posts, bollards, parking signs. Echo-location. Kilpatrick saw himself sitting outside a Belfast café, the blind man inclining his head towards him as he lit a cigarette; he supposed the blind man had heard the rasp of the flint lighter. Kilpatrick had not thought of Belfast since he had come to Paris – what was it, ten days, a fortnight ago? A month? It seemed like another world, the person he had been in Belfast someone else. Kilpatrick saw himself in his mind's eye as the man in the navy linen suit, the man in the Harris tweed jacket, the man in tan Oxfords or oxblood brogues, the man in the herringbone Crombie coat, the man in the camel coat, the man wearing this hat or that, as if all these men were other men; and he saw the blind man infallibly wearing the same outfit, a grey army-surplus anorak, jeans and white trainers, hatless, always the same man, reliably threading his way through the city with a sure step, as if he knew where he was going better than Kilpatrick knew himself.

Kilpatrick continued on slowly down Passage des Panoramas, blind to Passage des Panoramas. In his mind's eye he was in North Street Arcade in Belfast. Light poured in from the glass roof. He felt transparent, weightless. He would stop at a record store, a vintage clothing store, an art shop, a café. He would stop for a coffee before emerging into Lower Donegall Street and turning right, crossing the street and walking for some fifty yards before turning left into the archway that led to Exchange Place, where John Bourne had his studio. From the ticket pocket of his Donegal tweed jacket he would take out the old-style latchkey given to him by Bourne, unlock the heavy wooden entrance door and take the three flights of worn wooden stairs to the loft at the top of the building. As he entered Bourne's room Bourne would nod without turning round and say, Kilpatrick, I know your step. Bourne, Kilpatrick would reply. Bourne would be standing at the easel, a cigarette in one hand and a brush in the other, looking at what he had just painted. The floor of the studio was covered with what looked like debris, the contents of a skip, though Kilpatrick knew that for Bourne it constituted a resource: books, pages torn from books, Xeroxes of images, wrapping paper, swatches of linen and cotton samples, coils of old film stock. It was all grist to Bourne's mill. Kilpatrick would pick his way through the litter. He would stop and stand and look over Bourne's shoulder. What do you think? Bourne would say, and before Kilpatrick could reply, Bourne would step over to the butcher's block he used as a table, lift a boning knife and with two swift movements slash an X into the canvas. I don't like it, Bourne would say. It's not me.

10

THE LOST BRIEFCASE

———•◆•———

I am a displaced person. I inhabit the interlude between two movements, not knowing for how long. I am in limbo, the borderland between two states of being. After I left Beringer, I had made my way homewards, to find I had no home to go home to. A police cordon surrounded Elsinore Gardens. A police officer asked for my identity. I told him I was John Kilfeather. He informed me that 'a situation' had arisen at the Antrim Road shops – Video City, the Northern Bank, The Works Sandwich Bar, Zips and Rips Alterations and Dry Cleaning. I would be allowed back to my house for a matter of minutes, but was advised to take some belongings and to seek alternative accommodation for the night. How long might the situation continue? There was no way of knowing. Nor was I allowed to take my car.

The officer held up the length of white security tape. I stooped under and made my way to No. 41. I opened the door with my Yale key, feeling like an intruder. Already the house seemed to emanate an empty aura, the hallway almost alien in its familiarity. I packed a large briefcase with three shirts of various shades of blue, underclothing, toiletries, and a Muji A5 notebook. I also packed the typescript of $X+Y=K$. I could use this unplanned hiatus in my life to read it again and see what I had in mind all those years ago. I was almost out the door when it occurred to me to take my passport. I was abroad in my home city. On the bus into the city centre I took out the A5 Muji notebook. I opened the notebook at random. I found some pages devoted to Walter Benjamin, some of which I summarize here:

Walter Bendix Schönflies Benjamin was born in Berlin on 15 July 1892 to a well-off family of assimilated Jews. He was forced to flee Germany in 1933 and subsequently spent much of his time in Paris. In 1938 the Vichy government interned him for three months in the town of Nevers. He returned to Paris but fled Paris the day before the Germans entered Paris on 14 June 1940. He spent some time in the town of Lourdes before travelling to Marseilles, where he hoped to gain passage to the US. This proved impossible. In August 1940 he obtained an American visa to travel to the US from neutral Portugal. He would have to go through Fascist Spain, which could only be done via a clandestine route across the Pyrenees to the Catalan town of Portbou. He undertook the journey on 25 September at dawn. The path through the mountains was arduous. Benjamin, who had a heart condition, calculated he would have to stop every ten minutes and rest for one. He timed these periods meticulously with his gold watch. When he reached Portbou, exhausted, he found much of it still in ruins after Franco's bombing during the Civil War. On presenting himself to the police at the railway station, Benjamin was refused entry to Spain. He would be handed over to the French authorities the next day, and subsequently surrendered to the Nazi authorities. Confined to the Hostal França in Portbou, he took an overdose of morphine. On the morning of

26 September his dead body was found on his bed in Room 3 of the Hostal França. He was forty-eight. His effects were described in official documents as 'a leather briefcase, a gold watch, a pipe with an amber mouthpiece, a passport issued in Marseilles by the American Foreign Service, six passport photographs, an X-ray, a pair of spectacles, various magazines, a number of letters, and some papers, contents unknown.' Benjamin was rumoured to have been carrying another briefcase containing an important manuscript – the final version, according to some sources, of *The Arcades Project*. This briefcase was never found.

Upon reaching the city centre, I booked into the Adelphi Hotel in Ireland's Entry. A lifelong resident of Belfast, I had never stayed in the Adelphi, but had often drunk in its art deco bar, which was unchanged, it seemed, from the 1930s. I was assigned Room 7, which lay at the top of a narrow staircase. The furnishings, under the dim light of the dormer window, had the air of an even earlier period – a mahogany three-mirror dressing table, a mismatching mahogany wardrobe, a high oak bedstead, a bedside table with a night light, and a washstand with mirror. I went down to the bar. It was empty save for the barman and myself. I ordered a glass of John Powers and looked at surroundings: still unchanged. There was the alcove with three art deco mirrors on the wall, each flanked by wall lamps with bakelite stems, chrome back plates and frosted glass flame shades; there was the matching, facing alcove with matching lamps and mirrors.

I am sitting under one of the mirrors writing this in the A6 Muji notebook, referring sometimes to the A5 notebook, and from time to time I look up from my writing. I take off my hat, and see the man in the mirror simultaneously take off his hat. I hold up the pen in my right hand, and the Other in the mirror holds up an identical pen in his left hand. I take a sip of whiskey, and the Other does likewise with the other hand, we are countless men, our images forever receding and approaching in an infinite recession and progression. I am writing this with a Japanese Sailor Professional Gear pen with a Fine nib which corresponds to a European Extra Fine, about 0.5mm, and I think Walter Benjamin would have liked the Sailor Extra Fine nib, which draws, I would guess, an 0.25mm line – Benjamin whose famously miniscule hand could fit some hundreds of words on to a single sheet of hotel notepaper – Benjamin to whom the finest available nib was too broad, whereupon he would turn the pen around and use the back of the nib instead. I think of his notebooks in different formats and dimensions, crammed with writing – describing, annotating, cataloguing, speculating. I think of a sheet of buff paper found in his archive, headed with the emblem of Acqua Pellegrino, a blue-grey bottle against a red five-pointed star, on which he has written, or rather, this is an English translation of what he wrote: 'What is Aura? The experience of an aura rests on the transposition of a form of reaction normal in human society to the relationship of nature to people. The one who is seen or believes himself to be seen (glances up) answers with a glance ... When a person, an animal, or something inanimate returns our glance with its own, we are drawn initially into the distance; its glance is its dreaming ... Aura is the appearance of a distance however close it may be. Words themselves have an aura ... As much aura in the world as there is still dream in it.'

Above these words, to the right of the San Pellegrino star, Benjamin has written three lines at an upwards diagonal slant. In English, they make up eighteen syllables. A haiku, more or less? Knowing little German, unable in any case to decipher the tiny writing, I do not know if they are an accurate reflection of the original.

Eyes staring at one's back
Meeting of glances
Glance up, answering a glance

11

L'ASPIRATEUR

Kilpatrick exited Passage des Panoramas into Rue Vivienne. Here, as in Passage des Panoramas, were stamp shops and coin shops, and he thought again of Walter Benjamin's obsessive collecting – of stamps, picture postcards, books, children's toys, among other things. Kilpatrick himself had been a stamp-collector – philatelist, rather – in his teens, and intended to devote a section of his Paris book to those many shops which catered for collectors of whatever hue. He had transcribed into his notebook a passage entitled 'Stamp Shop', from Benjamin's *One-Way Street*, a text which Benjamin termed a notebook:

'There are collectors who concern themselves only with postmarked stamps ... The pursuer of postmarks must, like a detective, possess information on the most notorious post offices, like an archaeologist the art of reconstructing the torsos of the most foreign place-names, and like a cabbalist an inventory of dates for an entire century ... Stamp albums are magical reference books; the numbers of monarchs and palaces, of animals and allegories and states, are recorded in them. Postal traffic depends on their harmony as the motion of the planets depends on the harmony of the celestial numbers ... Stamps bristle with tiny numbers, minute letters, diminutive leaves and eyes. They are graphic cellular tissue.'

Kilpatrick walked along Rue Vivienne in a reverie, stopping here and there to look into a shop window. He saw himself at the age of fourteen or fifteen with a jeweller's loupe screwed into his eye-socket, scrutinizing a stamp. He would compare its characteristics to the description in the philatelists' bible, the Stanley Gibbons catalogue. He would mount it in his loose-leaf stamp album along with others of the set; underneath, in a calligraphic round-hand written with an Osmiroid italic pen, he would transcribe the relevant catalogue details. Like all collectors, he had begun with generalities, collecting everything and anything – the stamps of the world, in this instance. As he learned more he began to realise how much there was to learn. He bought books about stamps and borrowed books about stamps from the Belfast Central Library. He subscribed to philatelic journals. He learned to make ever finer discriminations, focusing on the stamps of the British Commonwealth, Great Britain and Ireland before specializing in those of Ireland and those of Victorian Britain.

Victorian stamps were ostensibly modest in appearance but bore a wealth of graphic detail. To the untrained eye, one Penny Red looked much like another, but they existed in hundreds of variations of ink colour, paper, perforations, die, plate numbers, type fonts, watermarks – shades of meaning that constituted a potentially vast field of study, not to speak of the abiding interest of postmarks, each recording a date, a place, the instant when a stamp became a used stamp. Some collectors specialized in stamps on covers, noting place of origin and destination in the context of the railway network of Victorian Britain. It was detective work, and, like Sherlock Holmes, these philatelists had frequent recourse to Bradshaw's railway guide. Kilpatrick was pleased to learn that in 1820 George Bradshaw, originator of the guide, had set up an engraver's shop in Crown Entry in Belfast, before moving to Manchester two years later.

Kilpatrick had visited Manchester in December 1968 at the invitation of Danny Fisher, an old school friend who now worked as a library assistant in the Manchester City Library. It was Kilpatrick's first time away from Ireland, and Manchester struck him as a Belfast constructed on a larger scale, with massive brick-built office blocks, hotels, derelict warehouses and factories some six or eight stories high, cavernous streets and black canals running between the buildings. It was three o'clock when he arrived at the centre, and dusk was already falling. As he walked down a sombre street, huge flocks of starlings wheeled above the glittering slate roofs, thousands of birds twisting, turning, swooping in perfect unison as if orchestrated by telepathy, and Kilpatrick imagined himself conducting them as he would an aerial symphony, waving his arms to synchronize their movements. He was unsure of his whereabouts. Many of the houses in the street were boarded up, and he was glad to come to the yellow light of a shop window where he got directions. He still remembered Fisher's address: 27 Bloom Street. He had not been in touch with him for years.

As Kilpatrick turned a corner he bumped into a passer-by. He muttered an apology and glanced up at the blue and white street sign: Rue Daguerre. He was far from Rue Vivienne. Lost in the past, he had no memory of how he had got there. He went into a bar café. It was still morning. The bar was empty. He ordered a coffee. The sound system was playing *Kind of Blue*. He lifted the cup to his lips. The track came to an end. There was a lull before the next track. He recognized it immediately: Glenn Gould's playing of *Contrapunctus XIV*. As he listened, he became aware of a hum in the background. A woman was vacuuming, the sound growing louder as she approached his table, drowning out the music. As if oblivious to his presence, head lowered, intent on her task, she vacuumed around his feet before retreating into the darkness at the back of the bar. The music was still playing, and he recalled Glenn Gould's anecdote of how, in his teens, he was learning Mozart's *Fugue in C Major* when the housekeeper came in and began to vacuum round the piano; on purpose, according to Gould. Gould couldn't quite hear himself, he said, but began to feel what he was doing, the tactile presence of the fugue as represented by finger positions, and also by the kind of sound you might hear if you stood in the shower and shook your head with water coming out of both ears. It was luminous, said Gould, the most glorious sound. It took off. He claimed that all of the things Mozart couldn't quite do, he was doing for him. And he suddenly realized that the particular screen through which he was viewing this, which he had erected between Mozart and his fugue, was exactly what he needed. As he came to understand later, said Gould, a certain mechanical process needed to come between himself and the work of art he was involved with. It was one of the great moments of his life.

The vacuum cleaner stopped. Gould's playing was nearing its end.

Kilpatrick had closed his eyes, bracing himself for the impact of that gunshot of explosive silence, when he heard a voice beside him. Wonderful thing, don't you think, said the voice. Music of the spheres. Kilpatrick turned round. It was the man he had met in the Irish bar, the James Joyce. Same red face. Black Hugo Boss overcoat. Black briefcase. It was the same man all right. If I may, said the man. He sat down beside Kilpatrick, and placed the briefcase on the floor at his feet where a moment ago the housekeeper had been vacuuming. Vacuum cleaner, what was the word? *L'aspirateur.*

12

ODD MAN OUT

———◆———

It has only just occurred to me that Ben, my watchmaker's moniker for me, John Kilfeather, is of course short for Benjamin; and the Flower Pot Man name, with all its associations with Flower Power and pot or dope or blow, Mary Jane, the Fragrant Weed, suddenly assumes, like a mantle, the scholarly aura of Walter Benjamin; I see that photograph of him, the hair rising from the high brow in a shock of convoluted waves shot with grey, one lens of the wire-rimmed spectacles catching the gleam of a contemplative or saddened eye, the thoughtful brow supported by the fingertips of the right hand, the strong nose above the drooping moustache, the lips half-hidden, his eyes of an inward cast not meeting the camera but entering an inner room where Walter Benjamin relives the memories of the man he has been and wanders again the boulevards of a foreign yet familiar city, lost and at home, or looks into the future; I admire the style of the dark jacket, the floppy-collared shirt, the dark tie with a thin diagonal stripe; and I see myself and John Harland looking at the photograph, which Harland had culled from a literary journal and pinned to a cork board together with a host of other images. It was Harland who had introduced me to Benjamin's writing.

He also who introduced me to the work of J.S. Bach, of whom I knew nothing, but presumed he wrote symphonies. Symphonies? said Harland. Never wrote a symphony in his life. Preludes, toccatas, choral preludes, fugues, Masses, oratorios, yes, but symphonies? Never, said Harland. I remember the first time I heard Glenn Gould's playing of *Contrapunctus XIV*, except I didn't know what it was then, I am still finding out, this opening statement followed by a recapitulation or development of what it bears in mind, a hesitant yet luminous exploring of the theme, which turns itself into itself by way of ever-branching variation, wistful sometimes, sometimes forceful, plangent, yearning. Harland had it on the Dansette record player in Exchange Place. All this time Harland was painting, jabbing or dragging or quavering his brush across the canvas in time to the music, leading the notes from the air to become the paint of the painting. As his body swayed to the music, I watched Harland become the conductor of things from one world to the other, I watched him become Hermes who negotiates the Underworld, Hermes the god of the crossroads, Hermes the god of chance, the angel who guides you to the page in the book you did not know you were looking for until you opened it, and looked into it.

Of course I didn't know then how the piece ended, and when it did, with that shock that still goes through me when I hear *Contrapunctus XIV*, Harland held his brush aloft in a final conductor's flourish, then threw it at the canvas. The hinges of form come about by chance, he said. Francis Bacon. He went over and perused the splatter the brush had made on the image. Interesting dendrites, he said. Nice axons. You know, the brain. I knew the terms vaguely. Clusters, branches, strings of nerve cells interconnected in some kind of fractal pattern, collecting and disseminating streams of information in the blink of an eye. I looked at Harland's splatter anew, seeing things in it I hadn't seen until then. But where exactly they were going, I couldn't say.

I looked up from my writing in the Adelphi bar, and found Paddy Ireland looking at me. Paddy was the barman. He was often ribbed about his name, but bore it with pride. He conducted his *métier* with professional grace and efficiency, and I see him now, Parisian-style in his black waistcoat and long white apron, brilliantined grey hair parted in the centre, silver armbands glinting in the crooks of his white shirtsleeves. Another one? he said. He knew me of old. He would know Harland of old. I nodded. We had just watched *Scene Around Six* together. The viable anti-personnel device planted by dissident republicans in a white Volkswagen people-carrier parked at the Antrim Road Plaza shops was being monitored by the security forces. Police were as yet unable to say when those residents who had been asked to leave their homes for their own safety could return to them. I sighed. Dissident republicans my arse, said Paddy. They're nothing but scum. Paddy was a republican of the old school of the forties and fifties. Dissident, I said, doesn't mean what it meant in East Germany, that's for sure. He set me up the drink and poured himself one under the counter. He raised it briefly to mine. To old comrades, said Paddy. Old comrades, said I.

I'm writing this in my hotel room. The Albert Clock has just chimed twelve, the way it does in *Odd Man Out*, and I think of the fugitive Johnny McQueen staggering, wounded, through the dark Belfast streets, puddles shimmering under gaslight. I've just smoked a little Black Rose. I blew the smoke out the dormer window. If you look into a flower head of Black Rose with a jeweller's loupe, you will see dendrites and axons of the glittering crystals that contain the active cannaboid ingredient, sea-salt white against the purple black of petal and sepal. I taste it on my lips and on my tongue. I had a sachet of Black Rose in my fob pocket. Lucky I didn't think of it when confronted by the policeman. It might have showed on my face, or maybe he wouldn't have noticed. He seemed fully focused on the current assignment. As it is, the room seems warm and hospitable in the dim light of the bedside lamp. I am writing the first thing that comes into my head into the notebook, and I think of Coleridge on laudanum, a few drops of the Kendal Black Drop taken in wine or brandy, Samuel Taylor Coleridge, STC or Ecstasy, as he liked to style himself, writing by candlelight in the dark cave of his library, discovering that words are coming to the page before he has conceived of them, his pen scarcely able to keep pace with their train of thought as they flicker forward like black candle-flame on the white page glowing in the candlelight, and I remember countless other times when I have written ecstatically in notebook after notebook, whether under an awning in the pouring rain or on the sunlit terrace of a café, scribbling for months, for years, circling round a theme that only gradually discloses itself, pages covered in words, arrows leading back to other words, words crossed out, addenda, corrigenda, pages flickering behind this page I write in now. I turn to Walter Benjamin. From the A5 notebook:

'He who has once begun to open the fan of memory never comes to the end of its segments. No image satisfies him, for he has seen that it can be unfolded, and only in its folds does the truth reside – that image, that taste, that touch for whose sake all this has been unfurled and dissected; and now remembrance progresses from small to smallest details, from the smallest to the infinitesimal, while that which it encounters in these microcosms grows ever mightier.' I place pen and notebook on the bedside table. I turn off the light. I go to bed. To sleep. Perchance to dream.

13

LA CHARADE

━━━━◆▪◆▪◆━━━━

Freddy Gabriel, said the man. John Kilmore, I presume? Kilpatrick nodded. Another coffee? said Gabriel. Kilpatrick felt trapped but there was something in Gabriel's manner that made him think he would not take no for an answer. Gabriel gestured to the waiter. *Deux cafés, s'il vous plaît, Marcel*, said Gabriel. *Ah, Monsieur Freddy*, said the waiter, and they embarked on some small talk about the weather. Gabriel's accent was impressive and the waiter laughed when Gabriel made a joke. Kilpatrick felt an urge to come clean. He had not had any kind of conversation with anyone for many days and he felt the need to talk like a normal human being. Actually, you know, he said, when we met the other day, I told you a bit of a fib. And he told Gabriel of how when you were abroad you felt you could be anyone, he knew it was silly, but he had momentarily succumbed to that urge to be someone else. His real name was not John Kilmore, it was John Kilpatrick.

Gabriel nodded understandingly. Of course, of course, old man, he said. Done the same thing myself. You're staying in a nice hotel somewhere, let's say Bratislava, ever been to Bratislava? Fascinating place. All go since the Soviet break-up. You're in this nice hotel in Bratislava, Hotel Arcadia, but no company, you're sitting at the bar late at night staring at yourself in the bar mirror, you've drunk a few glasses of the local schnapps, and there's a young woman sitting two stools away from you, attractive, well-dressed, you buy her a drink and you start talking, she's got fluent English, educated, you talk about music and art, this and that. That piece we heard just now, Glenn Gould? *Art of the Fugue?* You think she might be on the game, but she knows Glenn Gould, and you think, she can't be on the game, she's too intelligent for that, but then after a while there's something in her body language, and you know what? she is on the game, and one thing leads to another, though you have a great conversation before you get down to business, of course you don't tell her your real name, not that she expects you to, and you give her this story that you're a writer, you're thinking of setting a thriller in Eastern Europe, you know, it was half-true, I wanted to be a writer when I was younger, I wanted to be the next John Le Carré, I used to write awful pastiches of him when I was at Balliol, and we got into a pretty interesting conversation about the politics of the place, fascinating as you can imagine, and of course for all I know she doesn't believe a bit of what I'm telling her, but she goes along with the charade, and here are the both of you acting out your parts, and no one's the worse off for it. Kilpatrick nodded. He had been there himself, though all he wanted to do was talk, and he ended up paying for two hours' conversation.

We need to step into someone else's shoes occasionally, said Gabriel, or imagine that we do so. Kind of learning process. An enquiry into being. What is our nature? Why are we here? How can we attain virtue? How do we remember what we are? What is it Socrates says? All enquiry, all learning is recollection. You already know what seems unknown; you have been here before, but only when you were someone else. Platonic forms, and all that, we are but shadows of our real selves. And you, John, might I call you John? What do you do? I mean in real life? he said, tilting his head and smiling comically. Kilpatrick found himself taken by him.

Kilpatrick told him about his project, his Paris book that would include passages from French writers living and dead, matched to the relevant locations. He mentioned his interest in Patrick Modiano. Modiano? said Gabriel, wonderful writer. *Villa triste. Fleurs de ruine. Quartier perdu. La ronde de nuit. Rue des boutiques obscures.* Funny one, that, you know there is no Rue des Boutiques Obscures in Paris, though you think there should be, it's a translation of Via della Botteghe Oscure in Rome, not that Rome really features in it, so far as I remember. Kilpatrick told him he hadn't got that far, he had only begun the book yesterday, but it was certainly an interesting point, a typical piece of Modiano misdirection. And they talked about how Modiano's novels were often written in French *policier* mode, with a protagonist who might be a detective, and if not, behaved like one, except the subject of the investigation was himself. Not that there ever was a solution, or a resolution to the puzzle. But isn't that the way it is in life itself? said Gabriel, our lives have no resolution, there's no neat ending to whatever plot we think there is. There is no plot, you live, you die, and then others make up a posthumous story for you, that you won't know anything about, and if you did, you might not recognize yourself in it, you are not the man they say you are, you are someone else. Yes, said Gabriel, we live, we die. We do not know what happens next, in fact we never know what will happen next, living or dead. But we enjoy ourselves along the way, do we not? Every day contains a surprise, an unexpected pleasure. And you know what? Our meeting is indeed serendipitous. Unexpected, in the manner of all serendipity. We are two Princes of Serendip, you and I, he said in a mock-pompous voice.

And Gabriel announced to Kilpatrick that in his capacity as Cultural Attaché to the British Council he had organised a small soirée that evening, invitation only, at which the great man himself, Modiano, would be guest of honour. Would Kilpatrick like to come along? Do say you'll come, said Gabriel, I really won't take no for an answer, this meeting was meant to be, written in the stars, if you believe that kind of thing. At any rate it's happened. You'll enjoy the crowd. There'll be some Irish writers there, you know we in the Council like to maintain good relations with our Irish brethren. You'll find them good *craic*, isn't that what they say? He unbuttoned his coat and took a Mont Blanc pen from the breast pocket of his suit jacket. He scribbled an address on the back of a beer-mat. The suit was a navy pinstripe worsted, nice cut, Savile Row, thought Kilpatrick, maybe Huntsman. You will come? said Gabriel. Kilpatrick hesitated. But then, what had he got to lose? He longed for company. He smiled at Gabriel. I'm indebted to you, Mr Gabriel, I'd be honoured. Do call me Freddy, said Gabriel, must dash, one of those damn meetings, but yes, our paths will cross again tonight, 57 Rue du Bac, doorbell marked Vitrier, say you're with me, ta-ra! And with that he was off. He turned and waved his briefcase at Kilpatrick as he went out the door. Kilpatrick waved back. Kilpatrick took out his notebook to write down the address. It fell open at a quotation from Jean Cocteau. He couldn't remember which book of Cocteau's he had taken it from; in fact, he couldn't remember writing it, or where he was when he wrote it, but there it was, indisputably in his own hand: Since the day of my birth, my death began its walk. It is walking towards me, without hurrying.

Kilpatrick was disconcerted. But he could not dispute the truth of Cocteau's words. He walked out on to Rue Daguerre wondering what the rest of the day would bring.

14

THE FOLDABLE TRILBY

———•◆•———

I woke up. It was still dark. I groped for the bedside lamp. It was an old-style Bakelite lamp with a click switch on the column just under the shade at the base of the socket. My hand found the switch. The light came on. I was hungry. Aftermath of the Black Rose. I went to the washstand and splashed some water on my face. I replaced the towel on the rail and saw that the wall to the left of the rail was splashed with water that must have dripped from my hands as I moved from the washstand and groped for the towel. The water had dribbled on the wall in fractal rivulets like a root system or a river delta or a route map. I looked into the mirror and wondered how many other faces had looked into the mirror of Room 7 of the Adelphi Hotel, how many thousand other faces lay behind my face.

I was hungry. I dressed and went out on to the corridor in my stockinged soles. The corridor was lit by a single, dim, yellow, bare bulb. I walked to the landing. The stairwell was dark. There was a dimmer switch on the wall and when I pressed the button a light came on. As I came to the next landing the light went off and I had a brief, flickering after-image of myself descending the stairs. I pressed the next dimmer switch, and so on down until

I reached Reception. The night porter was asleep. I tiptoed past him and stooped under the hatch. There was a rack of keys on the wall and I lifted the one labelled Kitchen. I went in to the bar and over to the door which had a blue and white enamelled sign reading Kitchen. I opened the door. It was dark inside. I found the light-switch and the strip lighting flickered on. The floor was littered with swathes of paper, crumpled photographs, photocopies, manuscripts, fragments of plaster, everything covered in paint droppings, Cobalt Blue, Green Lake, Madder Carmine, Burnt Umber, and I had to pick my way carefully in my stockinged soles to the big yellow fridge in the corner. Naples Yellow. I opened it and the light came on. There was a platter with a turkey on it. One leg was missing. I tore off the other leg. I had put the leg to my mouth when I heard a footfall behind me. I turned and saw a man in a white overall coming towards me. He had a boning knife in his hand.

I woke up. The dream had been very real and I could still see myself in its other world. I got up and went over to the washstand and splashed water on my face. I replaced the towel on the rail. The wall to the left of the rail was splashed with water that must have dripped from my hands as I moved from the washstand and groped for the towel. The dribbles made a pattern I had seen elsewhere. Axons and dendrites. I went back to bed.

I woke up. When I went down to reception I was told the security alert was now over and that it was safe for residents to return to their homes. After breakfast I packed my belongings and took the 1F bus, Antrim Road via Carlisle Circus. I presented my 60+ bus pass to the conductor and took the stairs to the upper deck. The bus began its normal circuitous route through the city centre, Donegall Square, Chichester Street, Victoria Street, High Street, Castle Place, Royal Avenue, proceeding onwards up Donegall Street and Clifton Street to Carlisle Circus. Three white police Land-Rovers had blocked the Antrim Road and a white security ribbon fluttered behind them. The bus took a detour up the Crumlin Road. I felt a tremor of unease. The bus took another turn, past the jail. There was a bar on the corner, draped in Union Jacks and paramilitary regalia. I had not been in this district for a long time and buildings began to loom out of the fog of memory, shops, factories, warehouses, office blocks, some of them six and eight storeys high, some with ornate cupolas or Gothic clock towers, mansard roofs, dormers, parapets, domes, steeples, tall brick gables with faded, painted signs – Belfast Rope Factors Ltd., Cohen & Co. Auctioneers, Sun Life Assurance Company of Canada, Rollins Glass Designers and Factors Ltd., Standard Hemstitching Co., Imperial Picture House, Belfast Model Dockyard Co., Hebron Gospel Hall, Holland Wholesale Radio Factors, Melville & Co., Ltd. Funeral Furnishers and Motor Hirers ...

I had known these buildings from my childhood, but had forgotten them, and I felt both lost and at home, as if I were revisiting my past. I took out my notebook and was writing down the names when the bus turned again. From my vantage point on the upper deck I caught sight of a street sign. Berlin Street. I was definitely on the wrong side of the divide. Someone from my side could have walked these streets then, but not now. So much had changed, but the buildings, it seemed, had remained. The bus began to labour up a steep incline and the landscape seemed to tilt as if the bus was on a level. I didn't like where it was taking me. I decided to get off. I would make my way back on foot. I would keep my head down, making no eye contact. I had thought to take off my hat, fearing it would make me conspicuous. It was a foldable, navy felt fur trilby, Lock & Co. of London. I could have folded it and hidden it in my briefcase. But when I looked down at the crowd on the thoroughfare below, I could see that all the men were wearing hats or caps, hats and caps bobbing along, borne by the human current. I would have been a navy hat among many navy hats. Then I remembered that it did not matter, that I was to all intents and purposes invisible, in the way I have been on the streets of this same city, threading my way through the crowds on main thoroughfares, or walking through a portal into a narrow entry, where you encounter but few people, solitary men and women, the odd couple, or a street musician, the sound of his instrument amplified by the high walls. I am my invisible twin, the one I see in the mirror sometimes late at night, the other who is high on weed. A little Black Rose. Was it Bill or was it Ben? I feel the mirror neuron firing in my brain, electrical bursts of activity connecting from axon to dendrite to make me see in the other what I see in myself as I mime the other. I got off the bus and joined the human tide of the others, the people of the other side.

It was October and a fog was descending, the street lamps dimly coming on. The black cars parked by the pavement glistened in the yellow light. I put my collar up and pulled down the brim of my Lock & Co. hat; hands in coat pockets, I joined the throng, threading my way downhill against the flow. The road to be taken was becoming clearer to me. I saw the map in my mind's eye and the invisible fractal that would take me to my destination. I had not gone twenty or thirty paces when I found the crowds vanished from my orbit. I walked the pavement alone, past parked car after parked car, and something in me told me one of them was a bomb about to go off, but had not told me which one. They all seemed to be ticking over, when ...

I come to lying fully clothed on the bed in Room 7 of the Adelphi Hotel, my face under my hat. I take off the hat. I am awake at last. I am John Kilfeather.

15

THE YELLOW COAT

Kilpatrick walked to Montparnasse and took the Métro to Trocadéro. Montparnasse was not his favourite station, but it had a direct line to his destination, and at least it was not as labyrinthine as Châtelet/Les Halles, whose endless corridors he avoided if possible. He thought of Patrick Modiano's novel *La petite bijou*, whose protagonist, unusually for Modiano, is female. She is the Little Gem of the title. The first page finds her in the Châtelet Métro station, as I translate it:

'I was in the crowd on the moving walkway, going down an endless corridor. A woman was wearing a yellow coat. We were immobile, jammed against each other in the corridor, waiting for the gates to open. She was right next to me. Then I saw her face. The resemblance to my mother's face was so striking that I thought it was her ... She sat down on one of the station benches, away from the others who thronged the edge of the platform, waiting for the train. There was no room on the bench and I stood back a little from her, leaning against a ticket machine. Her coat had no doubt been of an elegant cut once upon a time, and its bright colour would have given her a flamboyant air. *Une note de fantaisie.* But the yellow had faded and had become almost grey...'

The faded yellow coat becomes a recurrent motif as the girl begins to follow the woman night after night, trying to establish the identity of the woman, which is linked to the girl's identity, the yellow coat flitting ahead of her through corridor after corridor, exiting a suburban station on to dark streets, entering telephone boxes or cafés, as the girl follows the woman in the yellow coat to an apartment on the fourth floor of a block of flats, night after night. Kilpatrick thought of the camel overcoat he had seen in Rue du Sentier and wondered if he would see it again. Freddy Gabriel seemed to have seen it in Boulevard Raspail; but then camel overcoats were not that uncommon in Paris. In any event Kilpatrick wondered if his memory of *La petite bijou* was accurate, perhaps he had exaggerated the multiple appearances of the woman's faded yellow coat. Perhaps he had merely had her wearing the coat in his mind's eye every time she appeared in the story, whether she was described as wearing it or not, and the coat was a memory of its previous appearances. The train stopped at Champs de Mars/Tour Eiffel. A woman in a yellow coat boarded the train. She sat down facing him. *Une note de fantaisie.* For a moment he thought of her as having stepped from the pages of Modiano's novel; but the coat was new, not faded to a near grey. Nevertheless he thought of the two of them as being somehow complicit as they travelled under the Seine to Passy and thence to Trocadéro, as if he had entered the novel himself.

Kilpatrick was bound for an exhibition at the Musée National de la Marine at the Palais de Chaillot, featuring Jules Verne's *Twenty Thousand Leagues Under the Sea.* He had read the book as a child, and it was one of the first films he had ever seen, in the old Alhambra Picture House in North Street. He recalled that underneath the Palais de Chaillot, which replaced the Trocadéro when it was demolished in 1937, was a huge aquarium built in a former underground quarry. He wondered whether to visit the aquarium or the exhibition first, and pictured shoals of exotic, brightly-coloured fishes, cobalt blue and emerald, turquoise, scarlet, yellow, gliding through the coral reefs of the quarry underneath his feet as he took in the Jules Verne exhibits. At the back of his mind, too, was an image from Marcel Proust, written while German Zeppelins and Gotha biplanes were bombing Paris. Dusk was falling, and the sky above the towers of the Trocadéro had the appearance of an immense turquoise-tinted sea, which, at low tide, revealed a thin line of black rocks, or perhaps they were only fishermen's nets aligned next to each other like tiny clouds. Then it was no longer a spreading sea, but a vertical gradation of blue glaciers, and the narrator thought of the twin towers in a town in Switzerland. Disorientated, he retraced his steps, but as he left the Pont des Invalides behind him there was no more day in the sky, nor scarcely a light in all the city, and stumbling here and there against the dustbins, mistaking his road, he found himself, unexpectedly, after following a labyrinth of obscure streets, upon the Boulevards.

On his arrival, Kilpatrick was disappointed to find that the aquarium was closed for renovation. The exhibition, too, was disappointing, held in a space made to seem larger by the circuitous route one had no option but to follow, doubling back into itself in a cramped labyrinth, tricked out with interactive computer displays. He emerged from the exit feeling cheated, as a young boy might from a tawdry fairground show. The only thing of real interest was a display of Verne's notebooks, written in a hand at least as miniscule as that of Walter Benjamin, must have been written with a crow-quill pen, thought Kilpatrick, on what looked like account books, the narrative adding up in column after column on the page, some passages colour-coded, with notes inserted in the margins, crossings-out, insertions, arrows leading back to previous sections of the text, a universe of detail, afterthoughts about those details, in their own way as impressive as the legendary galley proofs of *À la recherche du temps perdu*, the printed text snowed under by the blizzard of Proust's handwritten emendations and revisions.

To cheer himself up Kilpatrick decided to venture to Charvet in Place Vendôme, Charvet the makers of exclusive shirts and ties, cravats, *pochettes* in multicoloured silks; Charvet, where the rainbow finds ideas, as Cocteau said once. Kilpatrick remembered a tie he had seen in the window display once, a black shantung silk with orange and emerald green splotches. The price was beyond his means. He intended only to window-shop, but then again, perhaps they would have an end-of-season sale. He entered the Aladdin's cave of Charvet. Shirts were arrayed in back-lit alcoves, shirts of pale lavender and acqua and sky-blue, ties spread out on a dark mahogany table in a radiant colour wheel of blues, greens, reds, browns and yellows – paisleys, stripes, polka-dots in glowing silks and soft cashmeres. The impeccably turned-out shop assistant approached him, smiling. Monsieur. He held up his forefinger, went behind one of the glass-topped counters, and took out a long thin package wrapped in emerald green tissue paper. Kilpatrick was given to understand that Monsieur had been in the shop earlier that morning, had purchased the tie, and had asked for it to be put to one side while he went on to browse some more, but when the assistant had looked for Monsieur, he had gone. And when he saw him come in again in the camel coat, *le manteau fauve* ... Kilpatrick was about to demur. Then he thought, why not? He thought of the letter that had come to him that morning. From one John to another. He thanked the assistant profusely, put the emerald green package in his briefcase, and walked out on to Place Vendôme. He would wear the tie that evening to Freddy Gabriel's soirée.

16

BALL AND SOCKET

———•◆•———

I am still homeless. The telephone call to a local newspaper, accompanied by a recognized code-word, had indicated the general location of the bomb, a half-mile stretch of the Antrim Road, but nothing specific. The search for the device is ongoing. I am writing this outside Caffè Nero in Ann Street. I have just come from Miss Moran's tobacconist's in Church Lane, adjacent to Muriel's bar. I was running out of tobacco – so disconcerted had I been when evacuated from my home, I forgot to take the two spare packs of American Spirit I kept in the right-hand drawer of my desk. I thought of the empty house. I pictured the desk strewn with papers in the light of the art deco lamp, and myself sitting there rolling a cigarette, about to write some words. But then I would not be the person I am now. What I would write would not be this. There has been no bomb, and I have never stayed in the Adelphi Hotel. I bought the tobacco and wandered up Church Lane, into Bang Vintage round the corner, but such was my mood that I could not look at the clothes with any pleasure. I felt like a lost soul. I thought of the jacket I had bought there last week, in another world it seemed, 1960s chocolate brown hopsack with a faint charcoal stripe, Ivy League style, lovely roll to the lapel, nice drape to the material, I'd been looking for such a jacket for years. When I tried it on before the mirror it looked made for me. The shop owner knew me of old. It's very you, he said, when I saw it on you, I thought it was your own. I was pleased that he said so, though for all I knew he was giving me a sales pitch. And I too thought the jacket was very me, or what I would like to be. But today I do not feel as if I am very me.

I roll a cigarette. I have been coming to this quarter regularly for some years now, two days a week, taking the same route every time, and I see myself in my mind's eye retracing my steps again and again. I drive into Little Donegall Street and park the car in a cobbled yard. I lock the car and walk away from it. I turn right at the car park exit and walk past a windowless building, Shroud Manufacturers Ltd. Then a row of shut shops, their names and windows blanked by steel roller shutters covered in graffiti. Further on down is the cavernous loading bay of the *Belfast Telegraph* newspaper offices. Men in overalls are standing outside it smoking, others are unloading hay-bale-sized rolls of paper from a lorry. The street here smells of paper, cigarette smoke and exhaust fumes. Across the street is a nameless building, windows bricked up, formerly the Flying Horse bar, where I had my first drink, a bottle of Blue Bass. I cross the street and turn right, down Royal Avenue, past the Victorian neoclassical facade of the Belfast Central library, on whose steps I smoked my first cigarette, a John Player's.

I cross Royal Avenue; half the buildings are festooned with To Let signs. I turn left into Lower North Street, past the Northern Ireland Tourist Office, which occupies the site of the former

Alhambra Picture House, where I saw my first film, *Around the World in Eighty Days*. Some time in the 1960s it was converted into a Chinese restaurant, though still retaining much of the Moorish splendour of its interior, and I ate my first Chinese meal there in 1967, and visited it several times again before it was demolished after being fire-bombed in the 1970s. Today it occurs to me to take a little detour from my beaten track. I am about to make the short cut through North Street Arcade into Lower Donegall Street when I notice that the entrance is sealed by a steel roller shutter covered in graffiti, and now I remember, the arcade mysteriously burned down in 2004. Six years later the site remains undeveloped. As I take another route to my destination, Exchange Place, I see myself, as I have many times, entering Exchange Place to gaze up at the high mansard window of John Harland's studio, imagining myself floating up invisibly to glide through the glass and look over his shoulder at what he is painting.

He is painting me. I am seated before him in a Windsor chair. He is standing at the easel and he throws little glances at me from time to time, sizing me up, eyes darting from face to canvas and back again, or taking a step towards his palette, which is on a table between him and me. The palette is level with my eye. It looks like a landscape, pigments daubed and pushed and dragged into puddles and crests, mountains of emerald green and thunderous purple collapsing into carmine lakes, hillsides of yellow ochre, fields of violet. Beside the palette is a tray filled with curled-up tubes of paint. A name catches my eye. I stretch out and lift one of the tubes. Phthalocyanine Turquoise. Lovely name, I say to Harland, do you mind if I write it down? Write away, says Harland, you might want to look at the others, there's a phthalocyanine family, Green Lake, Blue Lake, Yellow Lake. And here's a nice one, Unbleached Titanium Dioxide, nice buff colour, I put a touch in here and there to damp down a stronger colour. I take out my notebook and begin writing. That's good, says Harland, keep writing, that's very you. And I keep writing as Harland paints, writing down what he says from time to time. I'm using an old canvas here, a trial run for another piece, he says, paint over it, I like working with a set of old marks, not to care too much. I like the paint to work by itself, with just a little help from me. Make a mark, see where it takes you. The hinges of form come about by chance.

I knew from of old, or in retrospect, that Harland was an admirer of the work of Francis Bacon. Like Bacon, he believed in happenstance, how what you are painting depends on the circumstances, what comes next. You never quite know how oil paint is going to behave. Different viscosity at different times, depending on the atmosphere, temperature, humidity. Sometimes the paint is slow to move, at other times it glides on to the canvas. Bacon, said Harland, believed in luck, or his own luck. When he lived in Monte Carlo he was obsessed by the casino. He'd spend whole days there, and he used to think he heard the croupier calling out the winning number at roulette before the ball had fallen into the socket. And he used to go from table to table. One afternoon he was playing on three tables, and he heard these echoes. And chance was very much on his side, because he ended up with sixteen hundred pounds at the end of the afternoon, an enormous amount of money for him then. Well, he immediately took a villa and stocked it with food and drink, though this chance didn't last very long because in ten days' time he could hardly buy his fare home to London. But it was a marvellous ten days and he had an enormous number of friends.

Harland took a step back from his painting. I think I'll stop now, he said. I'm at the stage now where I don't want to fuck it up, I'd be deliberating too much, and we don't want that. Accident, not direction. He took the canvas from the easel and held it before me like a mirror. What do you think? The image was a thing of daubs and patches bleeding or blurring into one another, but I had to admit he had caught something of me, some fugitive expression I recognized. It was very me, very John Kilfeather.

17

DOUBLE TAKE

———◆·◆·◆———

Kilpatrick could not wait to see the tie. He found a café in Rue Danielle Casanova and took a window seat. He unwrapped the package. The tie came encased in a mauve cardboard sleeve marked Charvet, and was further wrapped in a layer of tissue paper, mustard yellow this time. The tie was navy-blue herringbone silk with a muted orange diagonal stripe, and when he draped it on his hand the colours glowed and rippled in the sunlight. It would go well with the jacket he was wearing under the camel overcoat, chocolate brown with a faint orange windowpane check, William Hunt of Savile Row, he'd picked it up in TK Maxx in Belfast, down from four hundred to seventy pounds, he didn't know how they managed it. He'd wear it with a pale blue Turnbull & Asser shirt he'd bought in a sale in their Jermyn Street shop when he was last in London. He remembered the statue of Beau Brummell on Jermyn Street, facing the Piccadilly Arcade, poised theatrically with one hand on his hip, the other holding his hat and cane. One of those generic bronzes that seemed to be springing up everywhere to obstruct pavements, it looked nothing like Kilpatrick's mental picture of the Beau. But the pose reminded him of how, by all accounts, Brummell's style inclined towards pure theatre.

The neck-cloth especially, and how it was tied. The Beau's admirers would sometimes be invited to his dressing room to watch the procedure at close quarters. The neck-cloth was a triangle of fine Irish muslin, cut diagonally from a square yard and plainly hemmed. This was folded twice over at its widest point and wrapped carefully round the neck. Brummell stood at the mirror keeping his chin in the air before tying the tail ends in one of several manners. Each of these were in themselves signifiers of allegiance or taste. The next trick was to slowly lower the chin in a series of small 'declensions' that rucked down the cloth; the aim was to hold the contours of the neck rather than bulging out or folding inwards: a sort of self-sculpting, framing the face and defining the angle of the head. The folds emulated those in the clothing of Greek statuary. The line was understated, classical, seemingly effortless; the effect was nevertheless sometimes difficult to achieve. Brummell's valet, Robinson, was once noted coming down the stairs with 'a quantity of tumbled neck-cloths under one arm'. Upon enquiry, he replied, 'These, sir? These are our failures.' This too, was a manoeuvre, a piece of stagecraft. Robinson had no need to go out of his way to show the rumpled linen in public. He had been directed by his master to do so.

Kilpatrick stood before the mirror in Room 36 of the Hôtel Chopin, tying the Charvet necktie. For years he had employed a Windsor knot before reverting to the four-in-hand knot taught to him as a child. The Windsor was too square, symmetrical, bulky, the preferred knot of footballers. The aim of the four-in-hand was asymmetry, just that little bit of skew to give an air of nonchalance. The dimple, too, was essential, for without the dimple, the tie hung flat and inert against the chest, instead of making an elegant arch. Kilpatrick had spent months practising the dimple, spending hours in front of the mirror. Different ties required subtly different techniques. Different fabrics – wools, silks, cottons – had different tensile strengths. Some had better memories, held their shape better. Even now he had the occasional failure. But the Charvet tie knotted perfectly first time.

It is six o'clock and Kilpatrick is in the empty bar of Hôtel Nevers on Rue du Bac. He takes out the note the concierge of Hôtel Chopin had handed him earlier on. Forgot time, 7 at Rue du Bac, yours, Freddy G, written in Freddy Gabriel's flamboyant italic. The paper is expensive, cream laid, matching envelope. Did he give Gabriel his address? He must have done. Kilpatrick is seated in a dark alcove. On the opposite wall is an Egyptian Empire Revival-style mirror, elaborate ormolu frame, the glass tarnished, speckled at the edges. He sees himself darkly. He adjusts the knot of the Charvet tie. His drink arrives. Ricard, a little ceramic carafe of water on the side. He pours the water into the Ricard. He likes this moment of anticipation, when it turns from clear to cloudy. He remembers the old Regency Hotel in Belfast where Bourne bought him his first *pastis*, a Pernod. Kilpatrick had never heard of it till then, had never witnessed that transformation. When Bourne poured the water into the two glasses it looked like a magic trick. Why does it do that? he asked. And he gathered from Bourne that the alcohol contained insoluble particles of aniseed oil, different density to that of water. You add water to the oil, it won't dissolve. Instead it forms an emulsion. The light passing through the glass is scattered through internal reflection and refraction, that's why it's cloudy. Leave it long enough, it'll separate out again, the oil will settle to the bottom. Nice green, said Bourne, eau-de-nil. If you had a glass of Nile water it would do the same, you end up with a glass of silt and water. Like oil paint, leave it long enough and the oil floats to the top, the pigment settles.

Kilpatrick looked at his watch. A quarter past. He ordered another Ricard. He'd have another one after that, it would set him up for the evening. The drink arrived. A man walked in and stood at the bar. Out of the corner of his eye Kilpatrick saw the man glance at him. He turned away, turned back again and glanced at him again. He heard him ordering a Ricard. The man poured water into his Ricard, watching it go cloudy. Again he glanced at Kilpatrick. As he did so, it occurred to Kilpatrick that he knew the man from somewhere. He was wearing a blue and gold paisley scarf, black and white herringbone overcoat. He was hatless, going bald, sideburns, florid face, moustache. He searched his memory. He saw a thinner, angular man within the flesh – boy, rather, for he hadn't seen him since he left school, in what? 1967, over forty years ago. It came back to him: Chinese Gordon. Kilpatrick struggled to remember his proper name. Paul Gordon, that was it. Paul Gordon who was expelled for smoking dope, but then went on to Trinity to read Classics. He hadn't seen him since. The nickname was inevitable after they learned in history class of General Charles George Gordon, dubbed 'Chinese' after his exploits in the Opium Wars. Come to think of it, with the moustache he looked a little like his namesake now, in his old age. Kilpatrick rose from his seat and Chinese Gordon came over slowly to him. We seem to know each other from somewhere, he said. Yes, said Kilpatrick, Chinese Gordon,

I presume. Gordon laughed. Chinese indeed, he said, haven't heard that for years. And you, I know you, but for a minute I thought you were someone else, but you couldn't have been, for the someone else is somewhere else, I had to take a double take. You're, forgive me, it's been what? Forty years? Kill something, he said. You're Kilpatrick, John Kilpatrick. He extended his hand. And who did you take me for? said Kilpatrick. Oh, someone I met in Paris, said Chinese Gordon. You'd hardly know him. Calls himself John Bourne.

18

MORNING STAR

———◆———

We'll do another sitting next week, said Harland. I put the notebook away ... I wrote in the current notebook. I was pondering my next sentence when who should I see coming towards me down Ann Street but John and Jo, John Beringer the watchmaker that is, and his partner Joanna Leavey. Jo did face-painting for schools. They made a stylish couple, and you could see them coming a long way off, he in a slate-blue leather knee-length coat, nicely distressed, a green and red Tootal scarf at his neck, she in a 1960s navy check box jacket and a burnt orange silk scarf. I looked at my watch. It was nearly three o'clock; it was Wednesday, and I knew from of old that they took coffee at Caffè Nero around three on Wednesdays, regular as clockwork, you might say. We often bumped into each other accidentally on purpose. They had first met each other in Caffè Nero, two years back. She was sitting, pen in hand, doing the *Guardian* crossword. He was sitting, pen in hand, doing the *Guardian* crossword. As Jo lifted her eyes from the crossword, pondering a clue, John did likewise; their eyes met, and after that it was plain sailing. They'd both been looking at the same clue. And what was the clue? I asked, when I heard of this marriage of minds. Seven down, said Jo, Believe in the proposed route, say, in passing, 2,3,3. By the way, said John.

John Beringer, Joanna Leavey, I said. John Kilfeather, they said, what gives? So I told them the story of my displacement. And Beringer told me this story. It was what, twenty, thirty years ago, he was living in a flat beside the Waterworks. I was watching *Top of the Pops*, I'd smoked a bit of dope, he said, and I goes into the kitchen to raid the fridge and this blue flash comes out of nowhere, like sheet lightning, more of a flicker, the glass door of the kitchen blows in, then I hear the bang, there's been a bomb in the entry behind the house. I must have blinked or something, when I look again the whole kitchen's covered in this fine layer of dust, the colours are all bleached out, it's like some kind of simulacrum, you know, a projection from another world, the room's not the room it was before, I've just walked into another universe. So after a while the cops arrive on the scene, all blue flashing lights and sirens, and I'm out in the entry looking at the yard door, it's been blown off its hinges, I've just taken a drag of dope, and this cop comes up to me and asks if I'm all right, and I blow a lungful of Mexico's finest in his face, and I says, perfectly all right, officer, and he looks me in the eye, and he says, I haven't seen you, son, and he walks on. Good cop.

Speaking of which, said Beringer, anything on the go? Oh, the usual, I say, Black Rose, or there's a nice bit of Silver Haze if you like, nice mellow smoke, nice airy feel about it. So he orders half an ounce and we talk a bit about dope, and Jo says how she used to love looking into a flower-head with a magnifier, it was like entering a magic forest, and she talks pretty knowledgeably about THC and DBD, the high and the stony. I don't know Joanna that well, and I say, You seem to know your way around a flower-head, and she says, Yes, I know, the Little Weed, and why wouldn't I, I used to deal dope from the cloakroom of the Ulster Museum when I worked there. So she tells me how the client would come and leave his or her coat with her, payment in a designated pocket, take a stroll around the museum, and when the client leaves, the deal's in the same pocket. And she'd maybe tell the client to go and look at the John Lavery painting, you know, the one with Lady Lavery kneeling at a big window, there's aircraft in the sky over London, and to look at it sideways to see what they might see.

I knew the painting well. Back in the seventies John Harland had introduced me to James Conn, the Keeper of Art at the museum. Conn was going blind from diabetes at the time, diabetic retinopathy, they call it, but he held down his job for some years even when he'd gone completely blind, it seemed his memory for paintings had improved since he lost his sight, he could see practically every work he'd ever seen, in his mind's eye, he could still direct purchases when something appropriate came up for sale. And Conn told me to go and look at the Lavery some time when I had the chance, *The Daylight Raid from My Studio Window, 7th July 1917*, Lavery called it. It records the occasion when twenty-one German Gotha biplanes bombed London for the second time, the same Gothas that Proust had seen bombing Paris in *Time Regained, Le temps retrouvé*. Lavery's wife is depicted from the back, kneeling before a blackout curtain, seemingly observing the action. The blackout curtain is the key, you need to look at it sideways, said Conn. Look for a Virgin Mary, he said. I knew that Lavery, a Belfast Catholic, had indeed painted Hazel Lavery as the Virgin Mary on occasions, but I couldn't see its relevance to this painting.

So I went and looked at it. Sideways. And there, obscured by the putative blackout curtain, on the windowsill, if you squinted at it in a certain light, was a darker, keyhole-shaped patch, and when you looked at it with the Virgin Mary in mind it looked like one of those statues, Our Lady of Perpetual Succour, as if the kneeling Lady Lavery is praying to the Madonna in the hour of danger. Or mirrors Her. I remembered the Litany of Our Lady from childhood. Tower of David, House of Gold, Mirror of Justice, Gate of Heaven, Mystical Rose, Morning Star. So what's the story? I asked Conn. And I'm trying to remember what he told me, through the fog of all those years, the bombings, the drinking in pubs that were liable to be bombed at any minute, the blanks in memory, the obliterated buildings, the people who had died or disappeared, or who had been disappeared. I'd like to quiz him about it now, but he's been dead for years. I know the painting was one of a number Lavery gave to the Belfast Municipal Art Gallery, as it was then, in 1929. Like practically all public institutions in Northern Ireland, the gallery was run by unionists, some of whom, not to put too fine a point on it, were anti-Catholic. Did Lavery black out the Madonna himself? He was known as a painter of royalty, knighted in 1918. But then he had painted Michael Collins and Roger Casement. And the blackout curtain was a slapdash piece of work, not like Lavery at all, it was one of the things that had drawn Conn's attention to it. Was it the work of another hand? Whatever the case, a murky story lay behind this detail invisible to all but those who had been told what to look for, or to those who had, like Conn, looked carefully enough, without being told. There was no mention of it in the art histories. I'd never heard anyone speak of it again, until now.

So how come you knew about the Lavery? I asked Jo. Oh, I was in Paris, said Jo, can't remember what year, I met this guy in a bar, English accent, bit of a dandy, said he used to live in Belfast, John Bourne, that was the name, I remembered it, you know, because of *The Bourne Identity*, he told me about the Lavery. And there was something dodgy about him, I couldn't quite put my finger on it, as if he'd been spinning me a yarn, but when I got back to Belfast I checked it out, and he was right, the Lavery was dodgy.

19

A YELLOW BEAM

———◆·◆·◆———

So what brings you to Paris? said Gordon. Kilpatrick told him
his story. As for Gordon, he was with the Irish Diplomatic
Service, First Secretary to the Ambassador, with a special brief
for Culture. Had been in Paris for two years. Before that, in
many places: Colombia, Baghdad, El Salvador, to name some.
In Beirut he had been involved in the negotiations to free the
hostage Brian Keenan, who had travelled to Lebanon under two
passports, British and Irish – a dual nationality that might well
have been instrumental in his release, though there was no way
of knowing for sure. Kilpatrick thought of Brian Keenan, and
the other one, what was his name, McCarthy, John McCarthy,
an Irish name, though he was English, the pair of them chained
to a radiator telling each other stories to keep their spirits up.
Singing songs. What's that song of Dylan's, said Gordon, we
used to sing in the old days, back in Sixth Form? The keeper of
the prison, he asked it of me, how good, how good, does it feel
to be free? And Kilpatrick replied, And I answered him most
mysteriously, are the birds free in the chains of their skyways?
He thought of the vast flocks of starlings that wheeled over the
Seine at dusk, moment by moment changing from wisp of smoke
to tumbling cloud, bewildering the eye with the speed of their

movements. The same starlings over Belfast, over Manchester. Similar yet everchanging patterns.

But what brings you here, specifically, said Gordon, Hôtel Nevers? I don't think you got that far in your story. Yesterday in the James Joyce, said Kilpatrick, I met a man with a black briefcase. Before Kilpatrick could name the man in question, Gordon said, Freddy Gabriel, and he asked you along to the Modiano do. Of course you know Freddy Gabriel's a spy, said Gordon. Nice Oxford don-type spy, but still a spy, at least in a manner of speaking. Everyone knows he's a spy. For all we know he might be letting us know. Part of his game. That briefcase of his, for instance, hidden camera, mike. You can buy them online, for Chrissake. Everyone can be their own James Bond these days. Or think it. But as we know, it's not about the information. It's how you use it. Or what you think it is. What you think it's worth. It's about the deal. There's always something under the table. You have to ask yourself how well you know who's sitting on the other side. If they are who they say they are, or who they represent. There's always doubletalk. You watch the body language. They hide their hands under the table, usually they're hiding something. But then they might want you to think that. And then we have to ask ourselves who we are, and who or what we represent. Funny the way I took you for John Bourne. Some say his real name is Harland, but somehow I can't see him as a Harland. Much too practical, if you think of Harland & Wolff. And he laughed. Kilpatrick thought of asking if this Bourne might be the Bourne he knew, and as Gordon talked Kilpatrick was beginning to rehearse the story he might tell Gordon, but he thought better of it, and bade his time.

I guess I took you for him because of the clothes, said Gordon. Did you know that in the diplomatic service they train you to look at clothes? *Le style, c'est l'homme*, that sort of thing. Part of the cultural discourse. No, Bourne dresses like you. Or you like him. Dapper. The sort of man who thinks about textures and colours. And John Bourne has an uncanny feeling for such things, considering he's blind. Blind? said Kilpatrick. He tried to see the Bourne he knew gone blind. Yes, what is it, diabetic retinopathy? said Gordon. One of those things they diagnose when it's too late. You have diabetes, the blood vessels at the back of the eye start to leak. Anyway, Bourne can take a piece of material between finger and thumb, gauge the weight, the fabric, the colour even. Says his sense of touch has improved dramatically since he lost his sight. And he's become more intimately acquainted with the cut of clothes, he says. He can run his hand over a suit and tell to within a fraction whether it will fit. And then there's his painting. Painting? said Kilpatrick. Yes, said Gordon, Bourne paints. He was a painter before he went blind, and when he went blind he was in despair, I believe, but something made him get back into it again. Honestly, if you saw his work you wouldn't believe it was done by a blind man. I met him through Freddy Gabriel, of course, Freddy has a way of finding these characters, all part of his network. I think he thinks Bourne has some kind of extrasensory perception, sees things the normal person can't see, which makes him a good candidate for spy-work. You should talk to Freddy about him. *Un autre Ricard?* Kilpatrick nodded.

As Gordon went up to the bar Kilpatrick remembered Bourne talking about portraiture. What do we know of ourselves? he would say. Or of anything? Conscious perception is only a fraction of what we know through our senses. By far the greater part we get through subliminal perception. When I paint a face, am I painting the person I see before me, or the person I have in mind from all those times of seeing him before? Am I painting a figment of a figment? What do we remember of ourselves? A few fleeting fragments, which we make into shifting histories of ourselves. A kind of interior monologue. Sometimes we dramatize ourselves in the third-person. You know George Orwell's essay, 'Why I Write'? He describes how from early adolescence he made up a continuous story about himself, a kind of diary existing only in his mind. For minutes at a time, says Orwell, this kind of thing would be running through his head: He pushed the door open and entered the room. A yellow beam of sunlight, filtering through the muslin curtains, slanted on to the table, where a matchbox, half-open, lay beside the ink-pot. He moved across to the window. Down in the street a tortoiseshell cat was chasing a dead leaf ... and so on and so forth. I like the detail about the tortoiseshell cat, said Bourne. But anyway, the point is, through language we make up a fictive self, we project it back into the past, and forward into the future, and even beyond the grave. But the self we imagine surviving death is a phantom even in life. A ghost in the brain. As for painting what's before my eyes, said Bourne, sometimes I like to shut my eyes and let the brush take over.

Kilpatrick knew the Orwell essay, an apologia for his political writing. In a peaceful age, said Orwell, he might have written ornate or merely descriptive books; as it was, after five years serving in Burma as an officer of the Indian Imperial Police, a profession to which he was entirely unsuited, he was moved to write out of a sense of political injustice. Then came the Spanish Civil War. And yet, said Orwell, he never wanted to abandon the world-view he acquired in childhood. So long as he remained alive and well, he would continue to feel strongly about prose style, to love the surface of the earth, and to take pleasure in solid objects and scraps of useless information.

Gordon came back with the drinks. Kilpatrick and Gordon poured the water into the Ricard and watched it go cloudy.

20

LOCUS SUSPECTUS

———•◦◦•———

I'd forgotten my drugs. Medication that is. Some years ago, not too long after Harland disappeared, I had been diagnosed with high blood pressure. Subsequently I underwent an echocardiogram, familiarly referred to as an ECHO among the medical profession. In this procedure the patient is asked to undress to the waist and lie on the couch. An ultrasound probe is placed on the chest; lubricating jelly is placed on the chest so that the probe makes good contact with the skin. The probe is connected by a wire to the ultrasound machine and monitor. Pulses of ultrasound are sent from the probe through the skin towards the heart. The ultrasound waves then echo from the heart and various structures in the heart. I sat in the waiting area until the nurse called my name, John Kilfeather, and I went into the ECHO room.

As I lay on the couch I could see the sonogram of my heart on the monitor. It looked like a video of an alien planet, fuzzy with static, its chambers like continents expanding and contracting in time-lapse tectonic shifts; I could hear its movements, a coarse-grained rhythmic swash and back-swash as if of surf purling and collapsing on those alien shores, gathering itself for onslaught after exhausted onslaught; and I thought of how little we know of what goes on within ourselves, what phantoms wander the uncharted regions of the brain, unknown to ourselves. The ECHO showed I had stenosis, or narrowing, of the mitral valve which connects the left atrium and the left ventricle of the heart. I was prescribed a regime of drugs to lower blood pressure and increase blood flow. These included clopidogrel, atoravastatin, bisoprolol, amlopodine and perindopril, words that I have difficulty remembering. But I have the packets bearing the names before me now, having retrieved them from my home.

Home is where the heart is, they say. When I got off the bus at Elsinore Gardens the street was still sealed by white security tape and manned by a police officer. I explained my case to him; after pondering it, he held up the tape to let me through. Five minutes, sir, he said. As I stooped under the tape I heard the tap of a cane and out of the corner of my eye I saw the blind man coming down the Antrim Road, dressed in his familiar nondescript anorak, his long white cane swinging metronomically from side to side like the antenna of a mine-detector, and I thought how the white security tape had made a blind alley of the street where I lived. I walked towards my house, my home, feeling like one who has been away for so long a time that he has become a stranger. It was an eerie feeling to turn the key in the lock and enter the hallway, knowing that I had but a brief temporary access to the house where I had lived all my life, that soon I would be homeless again. Though I was in the house, it seemed haunted by my absence.

In retrospect I am reminded of Sigmund Freud's essay on the

Uncanny, and his teasing out the meaning of the German word *unheimlich*, literally 'unhomely', but translated into English as 'uncanny'; into Greek as *xenos*, 'alien'; into French as *sinistre*; and into Latin as *suspectus*, as in the expression *locus suspectus*, 'an eerie place'. *Heimlich* is 'homely'; yet, as Freud observes, there are contexts in which the word becomes increasingly ambivalent, moving from meaning homely, comfortable, tame, familiar, intimate, to secret, privy, inscrutable, hidden, locked away, removed from the eyes of strangers, until it finally merges with its antonym, *unheimlich*.

At the heart of Freud's essay is an analysis of E.T.A. Hoffman's story 'The Sandman', which revolves around the fear of blindness. Freud reads this as fear of castration. As a child, the protagonist Nathaniel is told in the evenings that he must get to bed because the sandman is coming, and on occasions he hears something clumping up the stairs with a slow, heavy tread. When he asks his mother about the sandman, she tells him of course there is no sandman, it's only a figure of speech, a way of saying that you're sleepy and can't keep your eyes open, as if someone had thrown sand in them. But when he asks his sister's old nurse, she has a different story. The sandman is a wicked old man who comes after children when they won't go to bed and throws handfuls of sand in their eyes, so that their eyes jump out of their head all bloody, and then he throws them into his sack and flies off with them to the crescent moon as food for his little children, who have their nest up there and have beaks like owls and peck up the eyes of the naughty children. Nathaniel becomes increasingly obsessed with this figure, identifying it with a frequent visitor to the family home, the lawyer Coppelius, a loathsome fellow who might or might not be the doppelganger of an Italian optician called Coppola, or of a Professor Spalanzani, who has made a female automaton with which Nathaniel falls in love, neglecting his sweetheart Clara. At one point he is assured by her that his obsession with the sandman is just that: perhaps there does exist a dark power, she says, which fastens to us and leads us off on a dangerous and ruinous path which we would otherwise not have trodden; but if so, this power must have assumed within us the form of our self, indeed have become our self, for otherwise we would not listen to it, otherwise there would be no space within us in which it could perform its secret work. This power can assume other forms from the outer world; but they are only phantoms of our own ego.

I was interested to learn that Hoffman was a Jekyll and Hyde figure: by day a respectable lawyer in the Prussian civil service, by night a user of laudanum, debauchee, and author of bizarre tales and satires. In 1819 he was appointed to the Commission for the Investigation of Treasonable Organizations and Other Dangerous Activities. Within two years he had written a satire on the commission that employed him; it came to the attention of the authorities, but proceedings against him were halted when it was discovered he was dying from a combination of syphilis and years of alcohol and drug abuse. On his gravestone are carved the words, 'Died on June 25th, 1822, in Berlin, Councillor of the Court of Justice, excellent in his office, as a poet, as a musician, as a painter. Dedicated by his friends.' He was forty-seven. The formal cause of death was given as *locomotor ataxia*, inability to control the limbs, or paralysis.

I take my medication: a tablet each of clopidogrel, atoravastatin, bisoprolol, amlopodine, and perindopril, and it strikes me that I do not know what these words mean. For the first time I read the accompanying leaflets, and learn that among the possible side effects of these drugs are dizziness, constipation, diarrhoea, anorexia, muscle spasms, nausea, nightmares, insomnia, hearing loss, fever, liver failure, blistering of the genitals, impotence, loss of memory, hallucinations, paralysis, and blindness.

21

UNE FALSIFICATION

The room on the first floor of 57 Rue du Bac was crowded when Kilpatrick and Gordon arrived. They stood on the threshold of the double doors. There was a dull thud, then another, and the buzz of conversation died down. Peering over shoulders, Kilpatrick saw Freddy Gabriel standing at a microphone, dressed in a navy-blue flannel suit, white shirt and burgundy silk knitted tie. He had a white carnation in his buttonhole. Beside him, on the closed lid of a grand piano, was the black briefcase and a half-filled glass of champagne. Gabriel tapped the microphone. Another dull thud. Silence. *Messieurs et Mesdames*, began Freddy Gabriel, and he launched into a speech alternately in French and English. The English, Kilpatrick noted, was sometimes a more or less direct translation of the French, but sometimes not, more an addendum or sidetrack. It transpired that Patrick Modiano was indisposed that evening, having been overcome by a bout of gastric flu. *Monsieur Modiano vous prie d'excuser son absence. Il est désolé*. However, said Gabriel, in his absence Monsieur Modiano has very generously granted his permission for me to read an extract from his current work in progress, provisionally titled *Rue Daguerre*. But first some words about the author.

Jean Patrick Modiano was born on 30 July 1945 at Boulogne-Billancourt on the outskirts of Paris. I cannot say why he chose to be known as Patrick, or whether it was chosen for him. But for the writer Modiano, whose work is engaged with a search for identity and its embodiment in language, the names are not without significance. Jean, or John, is the author of the eponymous Gospel, which begins, In the beginning was the Word; John the Divine is the author of *Revelation*; as for Patrick, the apostle of Ireland – and I am glad to welcome our Irish friends here tonight – many of the salient details of his life, such as his birthplace, are a matter of conjecture. By his own account he was born of Roman parents somewhere on the island of Britain, and taken as a slave into Ireland. He is an exile, and one could say that the protagonists of Modiano's novel are in a state of internal exile, forever searching for a home. Or searching for an absent father; we note that the name Patrick has its roots in the Latin *pater*, father. Modiano's own father is a mysterious figure ...

Here Freddy Gabriel embarked on a digression on Albert Modiano, originally Alberto, but known as Aldo. The Modianos were a family of Sephardic Jews from Modena, who had emigrated to Trieste, Alexandria and Salonika before settling in Paris, where Modiano's father was born in 1912. He discovered an early vocation for entrepreneurship – *très jeune, il se livre à des affaires et trafics divers*. Just before the Second World War he managed a shop selling stockings and perfumes. During the Occupation he evaded the 1940 Nazi census of Jews, living secretly under a series of assumed identities and involving himself in various 'business deals' – *escroqueries*. Among his associates was the writer Maurice Sachs ...

Here Freddy Gabriel embarked on a digression on Maurice Sachs. Maurice Sachs was born in Paris in 1906 into a family of non-practising, anti-clerical and republican Jews. His father, Herbert Ettinghausen, abandoned the family when Maurice was six. His mother, Andrée, was the daughter of the jeweller George Sachs. At the age of seventeen he ran away from home and spent a year in London before returning to Paris to live by his wits – *se débrouiller seul*. He worked as secretary to Jean Cocteau for a period, and was employed by the couturier Coco Chanel to set up her library; in both cases the relationships ended in acrimony due to Sachs's 'indiscreet behaviour'. In 1925 he was converted to Catholicism by Jacques Maritain and was about to study for the priesthood when rumours of his homosexual liaisons led him to abandon that course of action. In 1930 further indiscretions led him to flee to the United States, where he had a brief success in making radio broadcasts for NBC. He converted to Protestantism in order to marry the daughter of the moderator of the Presbyterian church of the USA. Three years later he returned to Paris accompanied by a young American actor he had met in Hollywood. In 1940 he made broadcasts for Radio Mondial urging the United States to enter the war against Germany, and was placed on a Nazi blacklist. He then involved himself in the black market and other dealings, helping Jews to escape to the Unoccupied Zone in exchange for money, and becoming a Gestapo informer ...

Kilpatrick looked at his watch. Out of the corner of his eye he could see Chinese Gordon doing the same. They caught each other's eye. I don't know about you, whispered Gordon, but I could do with another drink. Kilpatrick nodded. They slipped out. They emerged on Rue du Bac. They walked down Rue du Bac. A fog had descended and they walked from oasis of dim light to oasis of dim light under the streetlamps. Rue du Bac, Ferry Street, thought Kilpatrick. Fog rolling in from the Seine. The original ferry had transported stone from the quarries of the Left Bank to the Right Bank to build the Palais des Tuileries in the sixteenth century. Built on a site formerly occupied by a complex of tile kilns, hence the name. The palace had been destroyed by fire during the suppression of the Paris Commune in 1871. Fire, clay, smouldering stone ruins. It lay as a burnt-out shell until demolished in 1883. Some years ago proposals had been made to rebuild the palace in its former image, using the original plans and archive photographs. A magnificent simulacrum. Fake, if you like, what was the word? *Une falsification*. Kilpatrick remembered walking the Old Town of Warsaw, meticulously reconstructed after having been razed to the ground by the Nazis at the end of the Second World War. For all its period detail the area was drained of aura, the streets off the main square practically empty in contrast to the cacophony of the brutalist city beyond. It was like being on a film set. He was wearing a white trench coat and thought of himself as a detective who would find himself in a clandestine labyrinth behind the bland facades. Negotiations in dark cellars reached by darker stairwells.

Gordon halted at the corner of Rue Paul-Louis Courier. Where to? said Kilpatrick. I know a place, said Gordon. Les Caves des Changes, you'll like it. Sort of private club, don't you know, said Gordon, in order to be in the club you have to know about it, and not many do. Rules out practically everyone. Then it depends if they let you in. I should warn you in advance, and depending whether they let you in, that should you ever divulge its existence to anyone, you'll be barred for life. Of course I'm one of the several exceptions to that rule, otherwise I wouldn't be telling you about it, would I? I can introduce a candidate, but Les Caves reserves the right to refuse admission. Proper order too. And who introduced you? said Kilpatrick. Why, John Bourne, said Gordon, the man I took you for.

22

THE INFALLIBLE SCRIBE

———◆◆◆———

I am free to return to my home. On the midday Radio Ulster news it was announced that at ten o'clock that morning the security forces carried out a controlled explosion on the white Volkswagen people-carrier parked on the forecourt of the Antrim Road Plaza. It was envisaged that residents of the evacuated zone would be able to return to their homes that afternoon, and on the three o'clock news it was announced that it was now indeed safe for them to do so. When I arrive at Elsinore Gardens the forecourt of the plaza is still cordoned off, but traffic is flowing freely on the Antrim Road. Near normality has been restored. The forecourt is strewn with wreckage, twisted bits of metal, exhaust pipe, windscreen wipers, shattered glass. The car doors are scattered at different angles and distances from the body of the Volkswagen, like alien shields dropped on a battlefield. Behind the white security tape a team of forensic operatives are examining the ground. I stand and watch them. They are dressed in white hooded coveralls, white face masks, white gloves and white boots. I think of a Second World War commando film set in the Alps. I count eleven of them walking nearly shoulder to shoulder like a line of infantry. Their progress is painstakingly slow, their eyes scanning, covering the ground inch by inch.

Every so often one of them stops, stoops, and picks up something that to me is invisible.

Before abandoning my novel $X+Y=K$, I had done some desultory research into forensic science and remembered the phrase 'every contact leaves a trace', known as Locard's Exchange Principle, after Edmond Locard, the pioneer of forensic science who set up the first police laboratory in an attic room in Lyons in 1910. Locard established that we leave traces of ourselves everywhere, from our bodies, our clothes, our shoes – fingerprints, hairs, fibres, paper, paint chips, soils, metals, botanical materials, gunshot residue. The microscopic debris that covers our clothing and bodies, said Locard, is the mute witness, sure and faithful, of all our movements and all our encounters. Locard became known as the Sherlock Holmes of France; indeed, Locard acknowledged that he had been influenced by the fictional detective. 'Sherlock Holmes was the first to recognize the importance of dust,' said Locard. 'I merely copied his methods.' Locard was also a passionate philatelist, the author of several books on stamps, including *Manuel du philatéliste*, in which he devoted a section to the identification of forgeries – *les falsifications*. Locard applied his microscope to stamps as he would to the traces of a human being; stamps were graphic cellular tissue, from which whole histories could be deduced. The world was a series of correspondences.

I turn the key in the lock and the door opens. I enter the hallway and again I feel the house haunted by my absence, for all that I am here. The atmosphere holds the ghost of my breathing, smoke of cannabis and American Spirit; every room contains residues of the skin and hair and fingerprints of John Kilfeather;

everywhere are traces of my DNA, from which a future scientist might clone another me. I go into the parlour and pull up the blinds. A shaft of sunlight. The dust motes floating down through it are my remains. On the desk is my typescript of $X+Y=K$. I open it at random, and come across this passage:

'Everything receives the light that falls upon it, and so registers an eternal imprint of the things around it': this was the philosophy of William Denton, as articulated in his book *The Soul of Things*, published in Chicago in 1863. He was a keen student of the new science of photography pioneered by Louis Daguerre. 'We visit a daguerrean room,' says Denton, 'and sit before the camera; while thus sitting our picture is formed on a prepared silver plate, and is distinctly visible upon it; it is taken out of the camera, and now, nothing whatever can be seen; a searching microscopic investigation discovers no line; but, on a suitable application, the image appears as if by magic. It is no more there, now that it is visible, than it was before; all that has been done is to make visible that which already existed on the plate, or no application could have revealed it. Some will object that if the silvered plate had not already been made sensitive, the image of the sitter would never have been retained; but experiment has shown that this is not so. Let a wafer be laid on a sheet of polished metal, which is then breathed upon. When the moisture of the breath has evaporated, and the wafer shaken off, we shall find that the whole polished surface is not as it was before, though our senses can detect no difference. For if we breathe upon it again, the surface will be moist everywhere, except on the spot previously sheltered by the wafer, which will now appear as a spectral image on the surface. Again and again we breathe, and the moisture evaporates, but still the spectral image appears. All bodies throw off emanations in greater or less size and with greater or less velocities; these particles enter more or less into the pores of solid or fluid bodies, sometimes resting upon their surface, and sometimes permeating them altogether. These emanations, when feeble, show themselves in images; when stronger, in chemical changes; when stronger still, in their action on the olfactory nerves; and when thrown off most copiously and rapidly, in heat affecting the nerves of touch; in photographic action, dissevering and recombining the elements of nature; and in phosphorescent and luminous emanations, exciting the retina and producing vision.'

Denton knew from his own experience that the image impressed on a photographic plate could be extraordinarily persistent and difficult to efface; for, after polishing a plate once used, the figure of a former sitter would sometimes reappear, as if breathed into being, reminding one of the bloom that lies at the back of old mirrors, or a body seen through mist. He envisaged molecules streaming radiantly from the sitter to be received permanently into the depths of the plate. It followed that in the world around us, 'radiant forces were passing from all objects to all objects in their vicinity, and during every moment of the day and night were daguerreotyping the appearances of each upon the other; the images thus made, not merely resting upon the surface, but sinking into the interior of them; there to be held with astonishing tenacity, and only waiting for a suitable application to reveal themselves to the inquiring gaze. You cannot, then, enter a room by night or by day, but you leave on your going out your portrait behind you. You cannot lift your hand, or wink your eye, or the wind stir a hair of your head, but each moment is indelibly registered for coming ages. The pane of glass in the window, the brick in the wall, the paving-stone in the street, catch the pictures of all passers-by, and faithfully preserve them. Not a leaf waves, not an insect crawls, not a ripple moves, but each motion is recorded by a thousand infallible scribes; and this is just as true of all past time, from the first dawn of light upon this infant globe.' Nothing, according to Denton, is ever lost.

23

THE THIRD MAN

A black limousine glided up out of the fog, its fog lights on. It drew to a halt. A man emerged, attired in a midnight blue chauffeur's uniform. He opened the rear passenger door and stood to attention. Monsieur Odilon will see us there, said Gordon. Courtesy of the Embassy. Dear Old Ireland, as they say. They boarded the vehicle. The interior smelled of leather and tobacco. Kilpatrick sat to one side of Gordon on the long deep seat. We are twin passengers, he thought, two men who otherwise might have passed each other by, were it not for happenstance. In retrospect it had been preordained that they should meet, as if his thinking of Bourne had brought Bourne closer to him. He thought again of tomorrow evening's assignation in Rue du Sentier, and what it might imply. The Street of the Path. Or of the Track. The black limousine glided silently through the fogbound streets of Paris. Kilpatrick had no idea where he was and the idea came to him that he was floating down a dark river in the cabin of a motorboat. Mind if I light up? said Gordon. He pressed a button on his armrest and a panel opened to reveal a chromium ashtray. He took out a leather cigar case from an inside pocket. Vintage Dunhill, Kilpatrick noted. Smoke yourself? said Gordon. Well, I used to, said Kilpatrick, and you know, why not. Celebrate the occasion. Let me not be the cause of your downfall, said Gordon. On the other hand ... and he extended the case towards Kilpatrick. From our Ireland–Cuba connections, he said. Sancho Panza, maybe not top dollar, but pretty good. Bite or cut? he said. Oh, whatever you're having yourself, said Kilpatrick. With a magician's gesture Gordon produced an instrument and neatly snipped the ends of two cigars. He held up the cutter, snapped his fingers, and a lighter appeared in his hand instead. Vintage Dunhill again, nice art deco enamelled chevrons. Well, here's to us, said Gordon, and he grinned. They lit up.

Nice trick, said Kilpatrick. Oh, something I picked up in Istanbul, said Gordon, they're very into prestidigitation there. Like most magic, it's very simple if you know how. You'd be disappointed if I told you how it's done, so I won't. Some things should remain a mystery, don't you think? Some things, said Kilpatrick. And that's only speaking about the things we know about, said Gordon, what about the things we don't even know exist, that's an even greater mystery. Well, I'd like to know about Bourne, said Kilpatrick, the man you took me for. I used to know a John Bourne. You did? said Gordon. Yes, I met him back in the seventies in Belfast. He was a painter too. I met him in the Crown Bar. You remember the Crown? Sunlight falling through the stained glass windows of an afternoon, and you'd hold a glass of beer up to it and watch the bubbles floating upwards through the sunlight. And this afternoon I was sitting at the bar counter, Bourne was two stools away from me. Of course I didn't know he was Bourne then, but I couldn't help but notice his gear. Oatmeal Donegal tweed three-button jacket with the middle button done, navy-blue cord trousers, dark tan Oxford brogues. The light glinted on his sky blue silk tie. Nice jacket, said Bourne. He must have caught my eye out of the corner of his eye. I must have been wearing the chocolate brown cord jacket I'd bought a few days ago in the Friday Market. It was a nice jacket, vintage bespoke, made for a Dr T.E. Livingstone according to the label, I wonder what kind of a man he might have been, fitted me almost to a T, as it were. Of course I only say all this in hindsight. I don't think I appreciated clothes that much back then. I might well not have noticed the things I notice now. And I think it was Bourne who showed me what clothes could be, what they could do for one. And for all I know my memory of what Bourne was wearing has been skewed by what I saw him wear since. A notional ensemble culled from several ensembles. Anyway, I said, Nice jacket yourself, and we began to talk, we talked from afternoon till evening, said Kilpatrick.

By now the fug within the cabin of the limousine was thicker than the fog without, the faces of the two men briefly and intermittently illuminated by a dim red glow as one or other of them drew on his cigar. Insulated from the outside world, gently undulating with the dips of the road, the vehicle seemed to make no forward progress, as if moored between the banks of a dark river. Yes, said Gordon, what clothes can do for us. *Le style, c'est l'homme.* Though I believe the phrase originally referred to literary style, as if we clothe ourselves in language, which I guess we do after a fashion. Or disguise ourselves, for that matter. He drew on his cigar. Yes, he said, the old Crown Bar. I used to know the owner's son, back in the sixties, told me that under the brown paint of the ceiling it was all gold-leaf scrollwork, said Gordon. Is that right? said Kilpatrick, I didn't know that. I know they renovated it a couple of years ago, reinstalled the original gas lighting, but I don't remember anything about a gold-leaf ceiling. But it reminds me that that afternoon with Bourne I learned another thing I didn't know about the Crown Bar, you know the film *Odd Man Out*? said Kilpatrick. Do you know, I've never seen it, one of those things you mean to, but never do, said Gordon. Great film, I believe.

Well, said Kilpatrick, it's by Carol Reed, directed *The Third Man* too, James Mason is an IRA man on the run in Belfast, or a city we take to be Belfast, the character he plays is Johnny McQueen, ambiguous name or what, seeing he's against the forces of the Crown, Crown as in British, that is. I say he's on the run, hobble is more like, seeing he's been wounded in a botched payroll heist. At one stage he staggers into one of the boxes of the Crown Bar, and when I saw it, I took it for the Crown Bar, but Bourne tells me it was a stage set. An exact replica, every detail just so, down to the griffins on the doorposts, the brass match-strikers in the boxes, engraved MATCHES, the ornate mirrors. And you wonder why Reed went to those lengths, he could have had James Mason in some other less elaborate bar, he could have still called it the Crown Bar if it was the verbal association he wanted. Come to think of it, I can't remember if it's identified as the Crown in the film, said Kilpatrick. Maybe he just wanted to do it to show he could, said Gordon, an exercise in style. A piece of magic. Isn't that what films are about, making things appear to be what they are not? A forgery perhaps, but then forgery's one of those crimes we secretly admire, we all feel a kind of glee when the experts are fooled. We've arrived, by the way, said Gordon.

Kilpatrick had not been aware of the vehicle's stopping. The passenger door opened seemingly by itself. Odilon the chauffeur was poised at its side when they disembarked. As they did so Kilpatrick saw one of those massive oak-doored portals you come across in certain streets in Paris. Odilon retired to the limousine. Gordon went up to the portal and pressed a button on the intercom. It gave off a noise as if of short-wave radio. Gordon spoke into the speaker.

24

DOCTOR WHO

———◦◆◦———

The doorbell rang. I went to the front door. It was the postman. He gave me an armful of post. Three days' backlog addressed to John Kilfeather, 41 Elsinore Gardens, Belfast BT15 3FB, whether Northern Ireland or UK: letters, junk mail, packages. It was the morning after the day of my return to my dwelling place. Some show, said the postman, gesturing with a nod of his head to the street behind him. Three figures in white coveralls were shuffling at a snail's pace down the pavement on this side of the road, three others on the other, holding long white wands in front of them like blind men, one or other of them stooping from time to time to examine the ground in greater detail, sometimes picking up something invisible to me and either discarding it, or depositing it in a plastic bag; and I supposed they must be blind indeed to anything beyond their immediate field of vision, a matter of a square yard or so at a time, so concentrated did they seem on their task. I nodded back at the postman. In the time it took me to sign for some packages, bid the postman good-day, and turn to go back into the house, the figures in white coveralls had barely moved from where they had been. I took the post into the front room and took a Stanley knife to the three packages. I knew they were books. One bore the sender's name, Tgl Harmattan

2, Paris. This would be the Cocteau, *Tour du monde en 80 jours*. I couldn't remember what the others might be; I order many books online. As it turned out, one was *Three British Screenplays*, edited by Roger Manvell and published by Methuen of London in 1950. The screenplays were of *Brief Encounter*, *Odd Man Out*, and *Scott of the Antarctic*. I had ordered it for *Odd Man Out*, but the other titles were not without interest. I opened the book and found the first page of *Odd Man Out*. I rolled a cigarette.

This is what I read:

1. Passenger 'plane. A scene from a passenger 'plane which is above cloudbanks. The clouds drift past, and as the 'plane banks and then dives, the scene is momentarily obscured, until we catch a glimpse of a large city in a gap between the wisping clouds. Sunlight shines through the clouds which thin and finally disappear, revealing the great scene below, with mountains surrounding the city. We dive swiftly down and approach towers, smoke stacks, tall steeples and see everything in sharper definition. Then into view there comes a busy main street with traffic and pedestrians moving below, gazing into shop-windows. Dissolve to

I lit the cigarette, as I thought of it. As I smoked, the fog of memory cleared and I remembered the flying dreams of my childhood, when I would soar and swoop over Belfast, diving swiftly down and gliding along Royal Avenue at rooftop height, then just above head height. It is 1950-something, and I float above a bobbing sea of hats and caps. I am invisible to the crowds that throng the street, walking purposefully or aimlessly or gazing into shop windows and I do not know whether I am remembering a dream or daydreaming in the here and now, making it up as I go along. I take another draw of the roll-up and pause to hover at the window of Burton's the Tailor, admiring the three-piece navy herringbone suit displayed on a headless mannequin. Three buttons, narrow lapels, narrow trouser cuffs, it must be the late 1960s now. Gone for a Burton, as in dead, the suit you are laid out in when your time comes. I know that Burton's, where I got my first proper suit, is long since gone. So is the suit, into what oubliette I do not know. I'm daydreaming now, remembering. I'm coming on eighteen. This will be a birthday suit, so to speak. My father is standing outside the cubicle where I am being measured behind the drawn curtain: chest, shoulders, arms, waist, leg, the tailor deploying his tape with practised ease, jotting down my details in a notebook. I am in his book now, the suit already beginning to take shape in his mind's eye.

I feel slightly stoned. I lay the book on the desk and see a rolled cigarette beside it. I realize I am stoned. Only now do I get the scent of the Black Rose. Now I remember I'd rolled a joint just before my forced evacuation, and left it lying on the desk in my distraction. I am smoking a joint not the cigarette I've just rolled. I put it down to a happy accident. I'm beginning to see everything in sharper definition. I flick through the screenplay at random. Facing page 96 is a black and white still, captioned 'SCENE 156: Shell realizes that Johnny is hidden in the Bar of the Four Winds'. Of course. The Four Winds. I remember that John Buchan, author of *The Thirty-Nine Steps*, made into a film by Alfred Hitchcock, also wrote *The House of the Four Winds*, a book I've never read, and I wonder if Carol Reed had it in mind when he renamed the Crown Bar. I think of the four points of the compass, and then of the Morning Star, whose sign is a compass rose or star, and again I remember that October afternoon which seems a life ago, the thunderstorm, and rain spattering the pages of the missing notebook.

I look at the still. The character known as Shell, attired in shabby overcoat, scarf and bowler hat, is in the immediate foreground, glancing suspiciously to his right at something or someone out of shot. There are some twenty other men in the bar, many of them wearing hats or flat caps. Four of them, wearing white mackintoshes, look like detectives but are most likely not. It's just what men wore back then, in 1947. Behind the bar is the chief barman, played by William Hartnell, who later went on to play the first Doctor Who. What was his name? Fencie, that was it. Implication of illicit dealings. The fence who sells on stolen goods, which are under defence of secrecy. As I write I hear the menacing bass throb of the *Dr Who* theme reverberating in my memory. I'm writing this directly on to the computer now, having strayed somewhat from the notebook entry I'd made previously, what I had in mind to write. So I look up the theme tune on the net.

The tune was composed by Ron Grainer and realized by Delia Derbyshire at the BBC Radiophonic Workshop in 1963. Grainer's score, written on a single A4 sheet of paper, was basic: essentially, just the famous bass line and the swooping melody, with simple indications for timbre and orchestration: 'wind bubble', 'cloud', and so on. Derbyshire's job was to put electronic flesh on the bare bones. No synthesizers existed then: the music was pieced together by hand-splicing tape loops of an individually struck piano string – *dub-dub-de-dum, dub-dub-de-dum* – and sounds from an array of oscillators and filters used to test electronic equipment. A white noise generator provided the hissing sounds as well as the 'bubbles' and 'clouds'. I click on Grainer's name and discover he also wrote the theme to the 1960s *Maigret* TV series. French accordion music evoking bistros, cafés, cobbled streets glistening under lamplight. In my mind's eye I saw the opening titles, the black Citroën police car driving through the rainy darkness, windscreen wipers ticking metronomically; and I entered a fictional Paris.

25

LES STRUCTURES SONORES

———◆•◆•◆———

The intercom gave off a noise as if of short-wave radio. The words that emerged from it were unintelligible to Kilpatrick. Gordon said some words in reply. There was a click, and Gordon opened the postern gate. They walked through a vaulted entrance into a courtyard. The fog had gone. A full moon hung in the sky and a fountain played in the moonlight. They walked through the courtyard into a stone-flagged arcade lined with statuary, mythological figures whose blank eyes seemed to follow Kilpatrick as he passed them, or else he felt them boring into the back of his head. You know the way you know someone's looking at you, he thought, you can feel the gaze, and you turn to look at them, but by this time their eyes have turned away. Gordon and Kilpatrick walked to the end of the arcade, shoes clacking on the stone flags. They came to a door and another intercom. Again the same procedure. The door opened. They entered. They found themselves in a dark vestibule. Watch your step, said Gordon. They descended a steep stone staircase into a cellar space. Strange, ethereal music was playing. Under a series of arches along one wall were alcoves lit by art deco scallop-shell wall lamps. Interlocutors leaned towards each other over the tables, holding a drink in one hand and a cigarette in the other. Kilpatrick could make nothing of their murmuring. He recalled how often he had sat in other bars, overhearing snippets of talk drifting in and out of the buzz, trying to guess or make up whatever story lay behind this stray phrase or that, disembodied from whatever context, words like enigmatic messages emanating from a badly-tuned short-wave radio awash with static. Sometimes he would scrawl what he had heard in a notebook. Sometimes when he looked at it again in the light of day he would find his own writing indecipherable, or else he could not think of the significance of the words and why he had written them.

At other times he liked it when he was the only customer in the bar, alone with his own thoughts as they came to him over a martini or a Manhattan. He remembered the Blue Room of the Adelphi Hotel in Belfast, where at a certain hour of the early evening he would find himself the only audient to the jazz piano in the corner, not counting the barman, who had no doubt heard it all before as a matter of routine. Kilpatrick liked to think that this time it was different, for when he had seated himself, the piano player – a gentleman of a certain age, brilliantined hair, white tuxedo, cigarette smouldering in an ashtray – would give him a nod of acknowledgement or recognition and seem to launch into another mode, fingers lingering over the keyboard in a reverie of contemplation, exploring the contours of a song that was no doubt long familiar to him, but never realized in this manner until now, the melody haunting itself in its ever-changing repetitions, variations intertwining, unfolding, recapitulating till they dwindled to a conclusion by no means foregone. After the second or third song Kilpatrick would nod to the barman and the barman would set up whatever the piano player was drinking. They never spoke.

Absinthe, said Gordon. Two bubble-stemmed glasses and a carafe of iced water had been set before them. An elaborately perforated spoon holding a sugar cube rested on the rim of each glass. Louche, said Gordon. He gently poured water over the sugar cube and as the sugar dissolved the emerald liquid in the bubble slowly turned a paler opalescent. Kilpatrick, never having done this before, did likewise. Louche? said Kilpatrick. French for that effect, they call it *la louche*, said Gordon, where it goes milky. Opaque that is, and of course shady as in dodgy, not above board, shifty, sinister, whatever you're having yourself. He turned his eyes up as if quoting from an invisible text. The first stage is like ordinary drinking, the second when you begin to see monstrous and cruel things, but if you can persevere you will enter in upon the third stage where you see what you want to see, wonderful, curious things. Oscar Wilde. The element of water, said Gordon, liberates the essential oils from the spirit and releases the power of the *la Fée Verte*. Transformation has always been her fundamental essence. The Green Muse. The Green Fairy. Rimbaud's Poison. *Le bateau ivre. Le dérèglement des sens.* How would you translate that, the deregulation, the derangement of the senses? Whatever. *Santé.* He lifted the glass to his lips and Kilpatrick did likewise and he felt the absinthe cool and liquid on the tongue, burning as it went down. He thought of depths of opalescent green, emerald and eau de nil.

Kilpatrick looked around him. The other customers were all drinking absinthe too. They were talking more volubly now, as if they had turned their conversation down a notch when Gordon and he entered the room. They were elegantly dressed. He noted a lady in what looked like a Chanel jacket and a Hermès scarf opposite a gentleman in an impeccably cut navy-blue suit and a tie in black shantung silk with orange and emerald green splotches, colourful as an Oriental fish against the sea-blue herringbone ground of his shirt. The man fingered the knot in his tie and Kilpatrick found himself doing the same, fingering the Charvet tie that had been so mysteriously bestowed on him it seemed an age ago. He caught Gordon looking at him with a quizzical expression. You're wondering what these people are doing here, he said. Perhaps, said Kilpatrick, or wondering what we're doing here, if it comes to that. Oh, we're doing what they're doing, said Gordon, chasing the Green Fairy, being themselves, or rather one of their selves. Like us. Look around you, Kilpatrick. Kilpatrick looked around him and saw that every booth was occupied by a single couple not necessarily paired by sex. It's not what you think, said Gordon. Les Caves des Changes is about change, and to change one must become another self; so these people offer each other counterparts. The interlocutors play off each other as it were, reciprocating and elaborating each other's phrases, syncopating them as they would the musical score that is the sum of their parts, for they have rehearsed these words often in their memory, and they go back a long way, ever-changing as they move into the future or as time elapses. They are conducted by the mirror neuron, which reflects the words before they are framed by the conscious mind, the neuron firing a good few blinks of the eye before the phrase is even at the back of the mind or on the tip of the tongue; so they speak trippingly, pausing every now and then to consider what has been said, letting silence speak. They do not pretend to know each other, but go with the flow. The absinthe helps. So does the music. Listen. Kilpatrick listened to the ambient music he had first heard when he entered the room. He thought of tubular bells of wood and crystal swaying and chinking in the breeze through a wood as it blew through them, and the wavering of a wind-harp. He heard the birds in the trees. And he imagined John Bourne listening to that eerie music as Bourne walked through the forest of John Kilpatrick's memory, following him into the dark.

26

ACCORDING TO STRANGE

———◆•◆•◆———

With the accordion music of the *Maigret* theme still in my head, I opened another of the books that had come to me that morning, Jean Cocteau's *Tour du monde en 80 jours (Mon premier voyage)*. I had read no more than a few pages when it seemed to me as if I was reading a different book to that called *Round the World Again in 80 Days (Mon Premier Voyage)*, translated by Stuart Gilbert. So it proved. I took the Gilbert from the shelf and compared it to the Cocteau. The format and typographical conventions of each were, of course, different, but so was the sense.

Cocteau: ' — <<*Trente milles banknotes pour vous, Capitaine, si nous arrivons avant une heure à Liverpool.*>> *Ce cri de Philéas Fogg reste pour moi l'appel de la mer et jamais ocean veritable n'aura le prestige à mes yeux d'une toile verte que les machinistes agitaient avec le dos, pendant que Philéas et Passepartout, accrochés à une épave, regardaient s'allumer au loin les lumières de Liverpool.*'

Gilbert: ' "Sixty thousand dollars for you, Captain, if your ship makes Liverpool before one o'clock." In Phileas Fogg's appeal I still hear the call of the sea. Never for me will any real ocean have the glamour of that sheet of green canvas, heaved on the back of the Châtelet stage-hands crawling like caterpillars beneath it, while Phileas and Passepartout from the dismantled hull watch the lights of Liverpool twinkling in the distance.'

There are no caterpillars in Cocteau's French. And the end of the sentence, should, I think, read something like 'while Phileas and Passepartout, hanging on to a wreck, watch the lights of Liverpool coming on in the distance.' Nevertheless I had been beguiled by Gilbert's translation when I first read it on the Dublin train. The caterpillars are a stroke of wayward genius. As I look at it now, I am especially taken by his translation of *prestige* as 'glamour'. According to the OED, the primary meaning of the English word prestige (French from Latin *praestigium* illusion, as in prestidigitation) is 'a conjuring trick; a deception; an imposture'; the sense of 'influence, reputation, or popular esteem' comes later. 'Glamour', in modern English, is a shade different to 'prestige'; but its primary meaning is 'magic, enchantment'. It is a variant of 'grammar', harking back to a time when the study of language, in its incantation of declension, was seen as a magical art. A kind of hocus-pocus. For Cocteau, as he voyages across the globe, everything is glamour and theatre, or an opium dream. In Hong Kong, the streets recall the wings of a stage set; the shops and open windows might be dressing rooms in which consummate actors are putting on greasepaint before coming down to play their parts under the red and green limelight of the streetlamps. And as Cocteau leaves Hong Kong, Charlie Chaplin comes on board, bound for Hollywood. Chaplin has no French, Cocteau no English, but they converse effortlessly through mime, *la plus vivante des langues*, 'the liveliest of tongues'. Words become gesture.

Translation is the 'removal or conveyance from one person, place, time, or condition to another; the removal of the remains of a famous person, esp. a saint, to another place; the movement of a body or form of energy from one point of space to another; the action or process of expressing the sense of a word, passage etc., in a different language; the expression or rendering of something in another medium, mode, or form of expression.' And it occurred to me that reading is itself a form of translation, for every reader must interpret what he or she reads, visualizing the action or the scene described in his or her own way. The text is a series of stage directions, and we furnish the crime scene – the locked library room in a murder mystery, say – with the props of memory and genre, memories of real libraries we have been in and memories of other libraries in other murder mysteries. Each of us enters the room in the book in our own way. Each listener hears a different music, just as each of us is not only who we think we are, but the person seen and thought into being by others. Eyes staring at one's back. Meeting of glances. We are others in the eyes of others. I am many John Kilfeathers. I could feel the dope talking, so I looked it up, dope from Dutch *doop*, sauce, from *doopen*, dip, mix, adulterate. I thought of Dutch painting, colours mixed on a palette, scumbled into one another to become another, and the smell of oil paint entering the brain through the nostrils, down the neural pathways, reconfiguring the dendrite fractals in a fugue of variant and deviation.

Fugue is also 'a flight from or loss of the awareness of one's identity, sometimes involving wandering away from home'. I recalled the once celebrated case of Charles Burns of Belfast, County Antrim, a funeral director and a lay preacher. To all appearances he was a happily married man with a large and devoted family. On 17 January 1887, the day after his fiftieth birthday, Burns withdrew his life's savings from the local bank, and disappeared without so much as a word to anyone who knew him. After some weeks of ineffective police investigation, his family hired a private detective, John Strange, to look deeper into the matter; some six months later, Strange found him in Westport, County Mayo, working under the name of Cathal O'Byrne as the proprietor of a lodging house. However, when confronted with photographic evidence of his real identity, Burns refused to acknowledge it, saying he had always been Cathal O'Byrne and that the photograph bore no relation to his features. He immediately took the photograph from my hand, said Strange, and went over to the dining-room mirror. Looking alternately at mirror and photograph, he said over and over, How can you say this is me? I am not that man, I am this man that you see before you; and as he did so, said Strange, his eyes met mine in the mirror. There was an uncanny light in them, as if someone else was looking out through those eyes. It sent quite a chill through me, said Strange. According to Strange, Burns expressed a horror of his alleged existence as a funeral director, saying that he was perfectly happy catering to the living; indeed, he was a popular figure in Westport, and all who knew Cathal O'Byrne testified to his good character, and the grace and civility with which he conducted his affairs. Strange sought the advice of the local constabulary, who, after consultation with their colleagues in Belfast, corroborated that this was indeed Charles Burns, late of Belfast. The good news was telegraphed to the family. It was decided for his safety to confine Burns to a room of his own lodging house until the family came to reclaim him. Alas, when

129

they arrived, and the door of the room was unlocked, they found him dead. The body bore no marks of violence, self-inflicted or otherwise; he appeared to have passed away from heart failure in his sleep. It was, speculated Strange in his summing up of the case, as if Cathal O'Byrne, unable to countenance that he was indeed Charles Burns, had willed Burns to die. To sleep, perchance to dream. There were, he concluded, more things in heaven and earth than are dreamt of in our philosophy.

27

THROUGH A GLASS DARKLY

———◆·◆·◆———

Kilpatrick felt a tap on the back of his hand. Kilpatrick? said Gordon. Kilpatrick looked up and met Gordon's eyes. For the first time he noticed that they were green. You can stop listening now, said Gordon gently. Kilpatrick came to. Where was I? said Gordon. Yes, said Gordon, I was speaking of the interlocutors. The members of the club. As it happens, I picked up an odd volume of Emerson's essays the other day in Passage des Panoramas, and when I opened it my eye fell on a sentence that seemed very apropos. Library angel sort of thing, you feel some higher power has intervened. Call it coincidence if you will, but then in our line of business there is no such thing as coincidence. Anyway, essay entitled 'Clubs'. Discourse, says Emerson, when it rises highest and searches deepest, when it lifts us into that mood out of which thoughts come that remain as stars in our firmament, is between two. We apply that sentiment as a rule. Tête-à-tête that is. You spoke of a John Bourne earlier, said Kilpatrick. Ah yes, Bourne, said Gordon, a long story. Tell you what, why don't we do this in the spirit of Les Caves, said Gordon, you can tell me your story first, then I'll reciprocate. You did know a John Bourne in Belfast, did you not? Kilpatrick nodded, took a sip of absinthe, and began.

I seemed to know John Bourne before I met him, said Kilpatrick. I guess there would have been prior talk of him in the circles I moved in, so maybe that's how I picked up that impression. From elsewhere rather than from myself. We are wont to do that, are we not? And Gordon nodded sympathetically. At any rate when I did meet him, and really got to know him, I was beguiled by him, said Kilpatrick. About my height, about five foot eight, dark hair flopping over one eyebrow, somewhat sallow skin, a Roman nose a trifle too prominent for his face, ears likewise, he was not conventionally handsome, but he had presence, and when he smiled that broad smile of his, it seemed to illuminate one's own face besides his own. I first met him in the Crown Bar in the seventies, I spoke of it before. And one thing led to another. I became his friend, he mine. Perhaps everything seems inevitable in retrospect, but so it was. Why was I attracted to him? I can only answer, because it was he, because it was myself. We were each other's fate.

Your Bourne is an artist, you say. So is mine. I used to frequent his attic studio at Exchange Place in Belfast. Have you ever been to the Hugh Lane Gallery in Dublin? Some years ago the entire contents of Francis Bacon's attic studio at 7 Reece Mews in London, from the very plaster of the walls down to the floorboards, were removed and painstakingly reconstructed in Dublin, the floor ankle-deep in archaeological layers of printed materials, photographs, posters, champagne boxes in various states of decay, torn, crumpled or trodden on; everything, including the walls and door, spattered with paint, pots of paints and brushes here and there amid the chaos. When I visited the gallery last year I was forcibly reminded of Bourne's studio. One of the features of the Bacon studio is a big round art deco mirror propped on a table, the glass covered in hundreds of pockmarks where the silvering has degraded. When Bourne went to view the attic room at 14 Exchange Place, he was delighted to find in situ an old art deco dressing table with a round mirror similarly dimmed and pockmarked. I saw myself through a glass darkly, said Bourne. It confirmed that this was the place for him. He was very influenced by places, by the atmosphere of a room, and it seemed to him he had been here before, perhaps as someone else.

At any rate, when Bourne asked me to write a piece for the catalogue of a show he was putting together, I was flattered, said Kilpatrick. I spent long hours watching him paint, his eyes darting from subject to canvas and back again in a fugue of rhythmic glances, his eyes at times so narrowed as to appear shut, eyelids flickering as if in REM sleep. I see him now in his painting clothes, floppy-collared indigo denim workman's jacket, yellowed white flannel trousers, white boots, all spattered and smeared with a myriad of colours. When I remarked on the white trousers and boots, Bourne replied that he had once played a bit of cricket; they were relics of his varsity days. And I remembered that in the summer months he would often have the radio in the studio tuned to the cricket, one of those big old Echo, or was it EKO valve radios, ee-kay-oh that is, all hiss and static, Bourne would keep fiddling with the knob, but I gather that the bad reception had more to do with relative wavelengths than with any fault in the receiver. According to Bourne, light was the fastest wavelength in the spectrum, and given ideal cricketing weather, long bright sunlit days, it would interfere with the slower radio waves. And indeed, as the light began to fade, so reception would improve. The improved reception seemed to clarify one's inner vision of the match, and as I heard the commentators speak of what was happening, I could see the white-clad figures poised in their fielding positions on the greensward and the sun setting behind a bank of mauve and russet cloud; hearing the pock of bat on ball, I saw the batsmen flickering between the wickets. In lulls of play there would be discussion of the weather conditions, or the state of the pitch, where it might be breaking up as the fast bowlers further wore down an already worn patch for the spin bowlers to take advantage of. I knew little about cricket, said Kilpatrick, and Bourne's talk was an education for me. Cricket was a game of many dimensions including chance and skill. Temperature, wind, the ambient humidity of the air, all affected the flight of the ball. No one, neither bowler nor batsman, could predict how a ball might spin off a breaking wicket as it landed on a bump, hollow or fissure in the earth. It was the bowler's job to enlarge the parameters of unpredictability, to keep the batsman guessing. And again Bourne would quote Bacon, The hinges of form come about by chance.

So when I came to write the catalogue essay, said Kilpatrick, I used some cricketing analogies. Bourne had talked about cricketers of the past and how he used to try to emulate them. When he was a boy he read of how the great Don Bradman would, when he was himself a boy, repeatedly hit a golf ball with a cricket stump against the curved brick base of the family water tank, trying to anticipate the unpredictable angle as it bounced back, the boy Bourne copying the boy Bradman, except in Bourne's case it was an ancient garden wall covered in mosses and lichens. He dreamed of being Bradman, as if he remembered being him in another life, on the other side of the world. In sport as in art one learns by imitation; one can only be oneself by first trying to mirror another. Bourne was indebted to Bacon; through that emulation he had become someone he would never otherwise have been.

Most interesting, said Gordon. I am reminded of the *Meno* of Socrates, where Socrates says to Meno that all enquiry and all learning is recollection. You already know what seems unknown; you have been here before, but only when you were someone else.

28

BECAUSE IT WAS HE

———◆•◆•◆———

The accordion music of the *Maigret* theme faded. I could feel the Black Rose wearing off and decided to roll another. I keep my stash in a vintage Peek Frean biscuit tin with a bas-relief of a coral reef stamped into its lid, exotic multicoloured fish, sea anemones and urchins, the tin secreted in one of the drawers of the miniature burr walnut chest where I also keep my notebooks; and on top of the chest is a Bose Wave Radio/CD player which I bought some years ago, inveigled by the language of its advertising, reproduced in the accompanying manual, from which I quote: 'Extensive research in the fields of speaker design and psychoacoustics – the human perception of sound – led to the groundbreaking 901®Direct/Reflecting® speaker system in 1968. Acoustimass® speaker technology reshaped conventional thinking about the relationship between speaker size and sound, enabling palm-sized speakers to produce audio quality previously thought impossible from speakers so small.' And I thought of music resonating from the big wire grille of John Harland's EKO radio or from the suitcase-sized Dansette record player. I couldn't remember when I had last listened to the Bose. I switched it on, and recognized the sound immediately. It was Glenn Gould playing *Contrapunctus XIV*. I couldn't remember when I had last been playing it, but the display showed it had been some five minutes into the twelve minutes eighteen seconds of the track when I cut it abruptly short, well before the track itself comes to the staccato stop of its predestined, unfinished ending, followed by a silence like a gunshot. And I recalled how Bach's autograph of the music bore a note in his son Carl Philippe Emmanuel's hand saying, 'At the point where the composer introduces the name BACH (the notes, that is; in English notation, B flat-A-C-B sharp) in the countersubject to this fugue, the composer died' – a claim disputed by modern scholars, some of whom suggest that Bach finished the piece on another sheet of paper, referred to in the literature as 'fragment X'. But if fragment X ever existed, it has been lost.

When I had rolled the joint I lit it, turned the Bose back to the beginning of the track, and sat down to listen. How often had I listened to this playing of *Contrapunctus XIV*, ever since I first heard it in John Harland's studio all these years ago? I have no way of knowing. Many times in the studio itself, no doubt, and again I pictured Harland painting to that music, and tried to remember what might have then gone through my mind, or what had subsequently transpired that day, or on another. I had listened to *Contrapunctus XIV* many times on the car radio, sometimes immersed in it while I drove on automatic pilot to a destination I had been to many times, sometimes not fully listening as I drove an unfamiliar route; or I would find myself in a reverie prompted by the music, perhaps a fragment of a memory of being elsewhere on a previous listening, a landscape I had forgotten driving through until once more I heard the music I had been listening to then, a dark, nameless avenue without end. By now, after so many listenings, albeit mostly forgotten by my conscious mind, I have a fair enough outline of the piece, and can anticipate to some extent what comes next, and vocalize along with it, somewhat as Gould did himself; and as I do, I think how feeble my memory of the piece must be, compared to that of Glenn Gould, who could sight-read anything – whole orchestral pieces – and memorize on sight. He could read music before he read words, and had only to hear a piece or glance at the page of a score to retain it indefinitely, and I wondered if he could do the same with books.

Certainly, I could not; and, glancing around the shelves of the book-lined room in which I write, I wonder how many of these hundreds of volumes I could trace in my memory to their point of sale. Lately I have bought many books on the internet, but my library has come mostly from physical shops, many or perhaps most of them now vanished. And as I glance again, a ray of sunlight falls upon a stack of shelves, illuminating the many-hued spines of dictionaries, art books, novels, books of science and philosophy, books about books. My memory draws a blank with most of them. But here I see a row of vintage Baedekers in shades of faded red, and I remember, in an alleyway off Charing Cross Road in London, a second-hand bookshop specializing in travel books. On the shelf above is a *Robinson Crusoe* in an eighteenth century binding which I found in the Excelsior Bookshop in Smithfield, and I remember standing in the smouldering ruins of Smithfield after it had been firebombed how many years ago I cannot tell, remarking how difficult it was to burn books, for between the charred covers they still retained their inner core of text. And sandwiched between Jean

Cocteau's *Diary of an Unknown* and Paul Valéry's *Idée Fixe* is the three-volume Everyman edition of *Montaigne's Essays*, translated by John Florio, given to me by John Harland for my fiftieth birthday, or the day after it rather, for he had mistaken the date. From one John to another – Harland to Kilfeather, he had written on the flyleaf.

And I wondered again about the circumstances in which John Harland had vanished so mysteriously how many years ago I cannot tell, circumstances of which I was able to piece together some fragments over those years without ever coming to a conclusion. One thing was sure: he left knowing he was to leave, and never told me a thing about it. I only found out some months later when I bumped into an old school acquaintance – I cannot say friend – who had risen to some eminence in the legal profession, let's call him Holmes. We exchanged the usual pleasantries of two people who have not met for some time and would not care too much if they ever met again. I cannot remember how Harland's name came up, I must have mentioned it for whatever reason, and Holmes said, Harland? Yes, we all miss him terribly, said Holmes, took us all by surprise. And as the conversation developed it transpired that Holmes had received a note from Harland the day before he vanished, a note which said, Urgent business, will be away for some time, and that was all, said Holmes. Of course he was rather eccentric, said Holmes, and I nodded, and that was that. I walked for some time not knowing where I was and when I came to I saw that I had come to the door of 14 Exchange Place, which door I had tried many times in the past without success, until I abandoned all hope of seeing John Harland again. I had lost the key.

I lift the three volumes of Montaigne from the shelf, books that had been touched by Harland's hand. In my memory I undo a parcel of blue cartridge paper, not knowing what it might contain. Harland is looking at me and when he sees me smile he smiles too and it lights up the room. It is a very nice edition, 1928, the green cloth binding yellowed, more so now than then, with the passing of those years. I open a volume at random, and in The *Firste Booke* Chap. XXVII, 'Of Friendship', I happen on this reply given by Montaigne whenever he was asked why he so loved Steven de la Boitie: Because it was he, because it was myselfe.

29

JE EST UN AUTRE

<hr>

You have been here before, but only when you were someone else, said Gordon. As he spoke, the green wall lamps began to pulsate and the ambient music changed to a monotonous beeping. But hark! said Gordon, theatrically, lifting an index finger, the children of the night! And then, in a more soothing voice, Relax, my dear boy, merely our early warning system for one of those tiresome police raids, we get to know they're coming a good half hour in advance. We have our people everywhere, in all walks of life. They wear the appropriate uniform or garb, they take on the gestures and the speech of those whom they represent. Judges, bankers, art dealers, bookmakers, et cetera. The police of course. We have our friends in Quai des Orfèvres. If the world is a stage, they are consummate actors, becoming that which they are perceived to be. Only at night do they become that which they perceive themselves to be. We could talk about this all night, said Gordon, but for now, we can talk for as long as it takes us to finish our drinks. Gordon raised his glass. Kilpatrick reciprocated. As for what Gordon said thereafter, Kilpatrick, when he came to summarize it the next morning in his notebook, would have put it something like this:

Gordon said that in our walk through life we change, footstep by footstep, as irrevocably we are drawn towards our destiny and are altered by the glance of others. We glimpse a face in a crowd we think we have seen before, déjà vu or not, and we are changed by that apparition. We make our way through the crammed tunnels of the Métro brushing against or avoiding each other, and our bodies are altered by those negotiations whether we know it or not. A pickpocket sidles through the carriage and unbeknownst to you relieves you of something that was yours, and when you look for it you believe it to be lost by some inexplicable negligence on your part, or else you see in retrospect the man standing opposite you swaying sympathetically, his face buried in the pages of *Le Monde*, you remember how the motion of the train brought you for a split second into the most delicate of contacts, and the man pardoned himself as did you, you would never have revisited that moment had you not fumbled in a pocket and then gone through all your pockets for that which no longer was there, patting hip and breast as if conducting a body search on a person who was you. Gordon said that all our turnings cannot be otherwise than what they were, when we look at them or at what we remember of them in retrospect. With hindsight. And hindsight blinds us to all the other possibilities, which are myriad, said Gordon. And we are not one but many, we are the sum of all we are to others whether dead or living, for the dead have preceded us in our journey, and they have mapped out its territory in advance.

There was more in this vein which Kilpatrick could not remember. They drank the last of the green spirit and left by a secret staircase as the police were entering by another. They emerged on an empty street in Paris. It was dawn and a pale moon hung in the sky. The black limousine was parked some fifty paces ahead of them, engine ticking over. As he walked towards it Kilpatrick thought his footsteps made no sound as they glided over the pavement, or else Gordon's footsteps were so perfectly synchronized with his that both sounded as one. Odilon the chauffeur stood to attention holding open the cabin door of the vehicle. Kilpatrick boarded and Gordon followed him into the interior. Hôtel Chopin, said Gordon, Monsieur Kilpatrick will be tired after his long day. Had Kilpatrick told Gordon that he was staying at Hôtel Chopin? He could not remember. He sank into the long leather bench. Gordon? he said. Yes? said Gordon. You were about to tell me about John Bourne, said Kilpatrick. You are tired after your long day, said Gordon, we'll do something better than that. I'll bring you to see him tomorrow night. Would that suit your purpose? said Gordon. I regret I have another appointment tomorrow, said Kilpatrick. Ah yes, said Gordon, one of those unexpected invitations one sometimes receives when abroad. Surprise is one of the pleasures of travelling, is it not? But the night after tomorrow will be fine. Odilon will come to your hotel at seven o'clock and we'll proceed from there. Would that suit? Kilpatrick nodded. Suddenly he felt very tired and he fell asleep to the swish of the limousine tyres along an empty boulevard.

As he remembered it, he dreamed he was sitting in the front row of a picture house, waiting for the picture to begin. The auditorium was empty but for him. He was wearing a dress suit, opera cape and top hat. As the art deco wall lamps along the red plush walls began to dim he realized that not only could he see with the eyes under the brim of his top hat, but with another, disembodied eye that had no definite location; rather, it seemed the interior of the auditorium was all eye, or all camera, and he could view himself as he would a character in a motion picture. The proscenium curtains were still drawn when the picture began, superimposed on the red velvet pleats for a few seconds before they rippled open with a swish that was audible over the soundtrack, the same eerie music he had heard in Les Caves des Changes. He was watching a documentary entitled *Les Structures Sonores*. The commentary was in French and he could follow most of it with the help of the subtitles, his eye flickering in rapid movements as it registered the text. *Les Structures Sonores* was the collective name of the two composers, the brothers ... Kilpatrick could not remember their names when he woke but he knew from somewhere that Jean Cocteau had used *Les Structures Sonores* in his film *Le Testament d'Orphée*, or was it *Orphée*? In 1952 they reveal a new acoustic principle. They manage to amplify the internal vibration of metal and crystal. They make acoustic for a plurality of public. It is an ensemble of varying geometry. The sounds do not have the very precise frequency. For this reason, their combination is not organized according to their height but rather according to juxtaposition of tones. The rods, plates and strings are built on the amplification cones and rubbed, percussed or slided according to the non-verbal parameters. The elision and recurrence is another deliberation of technique. The structures are in many harmonies as you see in origami of metal. Kilpatrick saw on the screen a multitude of convoluted, multicoloured tubes and overlapping metal plates, shifting and swaying kaleidoscopically, somehow taking on the appearance of a tropical landscape in which the sound of rainfall on leaves and of waterfalls plunging into chasms mingled with the music, and he realized, when he came to write it down, that there were colours and shapes and sounds for which there is no language. He found himself in another terrain. He was struggling up a steep mountain path, carrying a heavy briefcase. He was out of breath and he wondered if he had forgotten to take his medication that morning. He stopped to rest. He took out his watch and looked at it. He rested for one minute as timed on his watch. He opened the briefcase and took out a passport and a pair of spectacles. He put the spectacles on and looked at the passport, and realized he was the man in the picture. A gunshot rang out.

30

OUBLIETTE

———◆·◆·◆———

I woke. I must have dozed off as a consequence of the dope. For a moment I didn't know quite where I was. I came to myself at my desk, left cheek on the open pages of the Muji notebook I'd been writing in, the Japanese Sailor pen in my right hand. I had been dreaming of John Harland, and, as I tried to remember the details of the dream in order to write them down, I suddenly remembered the Japanese box he had given me the last time I set eyes on him. He was wont to do that, present me with little knick-knacks from time to time: a netsuke tortoise whose head withdrew into the shell – fake, but very well done, he said, crafty piece of work; a Georgian silver salt-spoon; a lighter shaped like a miniature gun; that kind of thing. I see him now in my mind's eye, smiling as he stands before me in a blue cotton jacket, showing me his hands, turning them this way and that to emphasize their emptiness. He cups them, rubs them together, and opens them to reveal a small package wrapped in blue cartridge paper. He hands it to me with a flourish, and I take it. He has done this kind of magic trick on me before. The package is light in my hand. I smile, and nod. Don't open it until you get home, he said, and I left, and I never saw him again.

When I got home I undid the package. Inside was a buff cardboard box inscribed 'The Belfast Ropework Company Limited: Ropes, Cords, Lines and Twines'. When I opened it contained yet a smaller parcel wrapped in pale green crêpe paper, and on unwrapping that I found a small cardboard box with an interlocking labyrinth pattern on the lid. I lifted the lid and inside was what? I shook out the object and held it between thumbs and forefingers, examining it, turning it over and over to admire the complicated marquetry of what seemed to be a rectangular solid about one and a half inches by one by one. I looked again at the box in which it came and saw that jammed against the underside of the lid was a postage-stamp-sized piece of folded paper. I took a philatelic tweezers to it and teased it out. Unfolded, the leaflet measured some three inches by two, and I had to take a magnifying glass to it to read the tiny print of what looked a set of instructions. 'MAME' it began, 14-step Japanese Trick Box. But the more I read the more I realized it was a description, rather than a user's manual. I quote a little here from the text which is before me as I write. The mosaic and wood inlaid work a traditional handicraft are used. In this case, the marquetry and wood inlaid work serves as the pattern for the box; and it is thinly sliced and pasted on the box. This pattern also to maintain proper function of the trick box. The trickbox, with its advanced technological aspects, requires preseverance [sic] to manufacture. Despite this intellectually fascinating design and function, the trickbox is anything but mechanical. The feel and sound by which the tree runs are simple and gentle. This is the charm of the trickbox. 'MAME' is bean in Japanese. Under this last line Harland had written, From Harland to Kilfeather.

Underneath that again was a diagram of a box covered in numbers and directional arrows. I thought this might truly be the instructions. So I set about trying to open the box according to what little sense I could make of the diagram. Solid though the box seemed, it weighed too lightly for that. But the chamfered edges were smooth to the touch and showed no palpable means of ingress. I took the magnifying glass to it and could see no joins. I pushed and pulled at it every which way for a good half-hour, but for the life of me I could not get it to open. I tried it again three or four times a day for a day or two; again I failed, and I put it away in a place I forgot about, which I'm trying to remember now. I go through all the drawers in my room, from desk to cabinet to the two miniature chests, and discover many things I'd forgotten, but not the trick-box. I think of my procedures for putting things away, whether in a safe place, or too safe a place, or a thoughtless place, or somewhere I might identify later by some mnemonic, some incongruous but related image that might serve for the thing itself, a locus in the memory palace. I've been reading a good deal of French lately, and I think of a nineteenth century French-English phrasebook I bought in the market many years ago, charmed by the quaintness of its English as I had been by that of the Japanese leaflet – 'My postillion has been struck by lightning' – that kind of thing. I can see its faded gilt lettering glowing on an autumnal Morocco spine. But where exactly is it? I search for some time before I find it on a top shelf I have to take the three-step library ladder to. I ease out the book and crane my hand into the space behind, and find the box which contains the trick-box and the little leaflet. I take out both trick-box and diagram, trying to figure it out again. I turn the box over and over trying to find some purchase on it. Then unwittingly I do something or other I've never done before; there is a click, and I find an end panel of the box has shifted a fraction of an inch from its bearings. And bit by slow bit, sometimes backtracking and beginning again, trying this combination and that, I eventually crack the secret of the trick-box: a sequence of fourteen steps that turns out to be blindingly simple once you know how it works, each step leading inevitably to the next. Now I can do it with my eyes shut, for everything is in the movement, which is palpable and audible.

The inner compartment contains a miniscule scroll tied with the finest of threads. I open it. 41 Rue du Sentier, it reads, in a tiny nineteenth-century legal hand. And that is all. Intrigued, I put the address between quote marks and look for it on the internet. It is in Paris. Among the 54,300 results I come across a list of addresses of historical interest, including 41 Rue du Sentier, described as 'maison du notaire Jacques Ferrand, 1838'. Further investigation reveals that the solicitor Jacques Ferrand is not a historical person but a character in Les Mystères de Paris, a sensationalist novel by Eugène Sue published in 1838. This leads me to an English translation of the novel in which the house is described in some detail. It has a lodge, a garden, outhouses, and offices approached by a stone staircase, all in various stages of picturesque dilapidation. I turn to Google Maps and drag the pegman icon to 41 Rue du Sentier on Street View. A modest shop front in a narrow, empty street, it looks nothing like the house in the book. It bears no name, only the number 41 above the door. The blinds are drawn. As I pan along the street I know I have been here before, in the garment district, walking past window displays of bolts of cloth and tailor's dummies, I would have walked past No. 41 without registering it then. And I get that uncanny feeling sometimes generated by Street View, that one is actually there, a disembodied spirit roving along a street in the here and now, except it is not now, for the Street View photographs are continually outmoded by the present. There is a time lag. The Rue du Sentier I am viewing is no longer there. It is a ghost. And I picture Harland walking down that ghost street years ago perhaps, though whether it was his hand or that of another that was responsible for the scroll in the Japanese box, or whether it was magicked there from some other dimension, I have no way of knowing.

31

AURA

It was seven o'clock and Kilpatrick stood before the door of 41 Rue du Sentier. Earlier that day he had woken with a hangover, what was the French? *Une gueule de bois*. A wooden gob. Like a puppet, he thought. Nevertheless he had a clear memory of the night before, especially the dream, though he could not remember how he got home. Over breakfast he thought of how he might write an account of the dream, and made some perfunctory notes in the A6 notebook. Shifting kaleidoscopic patterns. Convolutes of intertwining tubes. He could see it in his mind's eye as if in a cinema, and hear the sounds of rainfall on the trees. On returning to his room he looked for his briefcase but it could not be found. He rang the concierge, who informed him that he had neglected, a thousand pardons, to tell him earlier that his briefcase had been left in reception that morning, courtesy of a Monsieur Gordon. Kilpatrick went to his room and opened the briefcase. He took out the A5 notebook into which he habitually wrote up the musings of the A6 notebook. He opened it to see a full page in a hand not his own, a neat miniscule that got a maximum of words into the line. My Dear Kilpatrick, it read, thought you might like to have this. You won't remember it, but you were talking in your sleep last night in the car, nineteen to the dozen, and I took the liberty of having Odilon record what you said. You were amazingly lucid, old man, I could almost see what you were dreaming myself, and I thought a transcript might be of interest you. So here it is, the only copy, for your eyes only; and until tomorrow evening, yours, Gordon.

Kilpatrick began to read and saw that it was so, that this was an account of what he had dreamed and how he saw and heard it. The sounds do not have the very precise frequency. For this reason, their combination is not organized according to their height but rather according to juxtaposition of tones, and so on, until he arrived in a different terrain where he became someone else, or else this was who he had always been. He saw himself looking at himself in the dream passport. He realized he was the man in the picture. A shot rang out. He took his own passport from the briefcase and looked at his photograph and his name and his autograph. I am John Gabriel Kilpatrick, he said. I am in Room 36 of the Hôtel Chopin in Paris, and I am writing a book which will feature extracts from books, fictional or otherwise, set in Paris, whether by writers living or dead, for the living writers would not write what they do were it not for the dead writers, whom they mirror, whether consciously or unconsciously. But I have been diverted from the path I thought myself on, and I find myself on another, which is proving interesting. Rue du Sentier indeed. He closed the notebook. His hangover had not entirely dissipated and he was still tired. He stretched himself on the bed and fell into a doze. He would pass the day at his leisure, have lunch perhaps in the Musée d'Orsay, perhaps taking in a little shopping before proceeding to his assignation.

152

Now it was seven o'clock and Kilpatrick stood before the door of 41 Rue du Sentier. By the light of the streetlamp he could see it was a plain shop front with no name above the door, just the number. He thought of an Edward Hopper painting. He took out the key that was in his pocket and opened the door. He went in and closed the door behind him. It was dark but the Venetian blinds were not fully drawn and lamplight filtered in though the gaps in the slats. He saw a desk in the middle of the floor and a man standing behind it. Kilpatrick made to greet the man before he realized it was a tailor's dummy. He went over and examined it. The dummy was wearing a tweed suit, English 1960s cut, brown herringbone with a faint orange windowpane check, jacket with slanted hacking pockets, narrow-cut trousers with turn-ups. He turned to the desk. There was a buff cardboard ring binder on the desk, and a handwritten note, which read, If the suit fits, wear it. He took off his overcoat and his jacket and took the jacket off the dummy and tried it on. It could have been made for him. There was a cheval mirror in the corner of the shop and he went over and saw himself darkly, turning this way and that to admire the way the slats of light fell on the windowpane check. He went back to the desk and opened the ring binder. It contained a substantial typescript. The first page bore the legend $X+Y=K$. He was flicking through the pages when his eye fell on the name Kilpatrick. His heart skipped a beat. He read a paragraph:

Macaulay, Kilpatrick's GP, had referred him to a Dr Holmes, whose premises at Alpha Chambers were located in the linen district. Gloomy Victorian buildings loomed above the damp pavements and the air was redolent with lint and coal smoke.

Even since before the War, the industry had been in decline, but whole streets still remained that were almost exclusively devoted to textile agencies and outlets – imposing offices of exporters in fine damasks, long blank-windowed warehouses, little dim-lit shops that specialized in things like yarns and threads, diapers, handkerchiefs, art linen. He had taken the tram to Corporation Square. From there it should have been only a few minutes walk to the Alpha building in Steam-mill Lane, but Kilpatrick's sense of the district was poor, and though he could see the entrance to the building in his mind's eye – he had been interviewed there some years previously – he could not properly visualize its whereabouts. As he took yet another wrong turn he heard the spin-cycle din of a surveillance helicopter overhead. Feeling the invisible ray of its telephoto vision on the back of his neck, he looked up briefly. It hovered motionlessly on the many-fathomed wash of its own noise, dispassionately recording his movements. At least *they* would know where he was going, he thought ruefully ...

As he skimmed the book further he felt a growing sense of bewilderment. Some bits were clearly fiction, but others chimed with his own memories, whether of his waking or his dreaming life. For example, the Kilpatrick in the book was prone to migraine, as Kilpatrick himself had been in his teens, and passages such as the following reflected his own experience:

Common to many experiences of migraine is the aura, a term first applied to the sensory hallucinations immediately preceding certain epileptic seizures. On closing the eyes, some patients experience a visual tumult or delirium, in which latticed, faceted and tessellated motifs predominate – images resembling mosaics, honeycombs, or Turkish rugs. These evanescent figments tend to be brilliantly luminous, coloured, highly unstable, and liable to sudden kaleidoscopic transformations. They are usually no more than a preamble to the major portion of the visual aura. Usually the patient goes on to undergo a longer-lasting and far more elaborate hallucination within the visual field – the migraine scotoma ...

The slatted light was beginning to give him the jitters. Kilpatrick closed the ring binder and put it into his briefcase. He needed to get away and think.

32

FULL FATHOM FIVE

———◆•◆•◆———

As I considered the implications of the Japanese box, I looked at my watch. It was nearly three o'clock, and I remembered I had to meet a client at four to show him a watch. Nice Omega Constellation, 1960, running strong. It was a bright and sunny October day, perfect weather for the Livingstone suit. But when I went to the wardrobe where it should have been, it wasn't there. I looked in the other wardrobes. Maybe I had stored it in the attic? I was still disorientated from the events of the past few days. I would look for it later, it must be somewhere in the house, suits don't just get up and walk away by themselves, though I did remember Lazenbatt the tailor saying the trousers could stand up on their own, or was that the Burton suit? Whatever. I settled for an oatmeal Donegal tweed three-button jacket, navy-blue cord trousers, and dark tan Oxford brogues that matched my briefcase.

I was almost out the door when I remembered I'd forgotten to take my medication. So I did, a tablet each of clopidogrel, atoravastatin, bisoprolol, amlopodine and perindopril. Reminded of Glenn Gould's prodigious consumption of pharmaceutical drugs – Nembutal, Luminal, Berutal, Valium, Librax, Indocin,

Naprosyn, and Aldomet, among others – I took his CD of *Contrapunctus XIV* with me to play in the car. When I turned on the audio I got a crackle of static and reckoned it must be in radio mode, and was about to switch to the CD player when I heard the words, *L'oiseau chante avec ses doigts* – the bird sings with its fingers – and recognized the phrase as one of the enigmatic communications received on the car radio by Orphée in Jean Cocteau's film of the same name, based loosely on the Orpheus myth. It seemed I was listening to a radio adaptation of the screenplay. In the film, the messages are transmitted from the Underworld by the young poet Cégeste, who has been killed by two motorcyclists, emissaries of a mysterious princess. Orphée publishes the messages as poetry and is accused of plagiarism. I heard another few fragments of dialogue before the radio emitted another burst of static. Then there was silence before I heard the phrase again, loud and clear: *L'oiseau chante avec ses doigts. Deux fois. L'oiseau chante avec ses doigts. Deux fois. Je répète ...*

The radio went dead. I twiddled the knob; but instead of the mysterious broadcast, a Radio Ulster news bulletin came on, announcing that a suspect device had been found in the vicinity of Corporation Square and that the area ... I switched to CD mode, and drove into town, listening to *Contrapunctus XIV* unfold itself, as I had so many times before, hearing different permutations in it every time, echoes overlaying other echoes. The traffic was slower than usual due to the putative bomb; but as it happened, the journey took precisely the twelve minutes and eighteen seconds of Gould's playing, for the music came to a stop with that familiar gunshot of silence just as I parked behind the Central Library: a happy coincidence that I thought augured well for the day. I had still a good three-quarters of an hour before my assignation. On a whim I decided to revisit Exchange Place. It had been some years since I had been there, but my thinking about Harland had become more productive of late, and I was sure the sight of the place would prompt new memories. As I entered the narrow entry I remarked, as I had so many times before, the cannon-shaped iron bollards that flanked the entrance, bearing the dints and dents of so many years of traffic. My feet on the cobblestones passed over the footfall of so many others, including my own, because I was someone other then: I did not know then what I now suspect. I came to the door of 14 Exchange Place to find it open. I entered. The vestibule had an air of disuse. I rapped on the door of Federman the stationer, whose depot took up the ground floor. I rapped again, and it opened to reveal the man himself, not much changed since I had seen him last, and still with a pencil in the breast pocket of the tan cotton drill shop-coat he'd worn ever since I'd known him. He threw himself back in mock surprise. If it isn't himself! he cried, returned from the dead, John Kilfeather, how are you? and he thrust his hand forward. We made some small talk before I came to the question. And Harland? I said, have you heard anything more of him? Well, said Federman, you know how I felt about him even before he took off, and nothing much has happened since to make me change my mind. But would you listen to me? And as I listened to him I knew that he was right. We had talked of these matters before at some length. But somehow or other I never thought of asking to see the attic studio back then, perhaps it was a matter of pride; I thought of the enquiries I had conducted as being casual and perfunctory, but in retrospect I can see that Federman would have thought otherwise. So I put the next question to him. But of course! he cried, I thought you'd never ask! And he went into the shop and came out with a key. Onwards and upwards! he cried, and I mounted the long, high, narrow stair to the attic studio, my passage lit by a skylight in the roof of the stairwell, my heart quickening with every tread.

I put the key in the door and had to jiggle it a bit before the lock gave. I entered to find the studio in what must have been the state that he left it in. There was the familiar chaos dimly replicated in the deteriorating mirror: crumpled images lying amid crumpled champagne boxes, layers of stuff that had been walked upon by Harland. I scuffled some of it about with my shoe, something I would never have dared to do before, when I tiptoed my way gently through it as I would through an precarious labyrinth. I looked down. The scuffling had revealed a pale blue cover like those of the school exercise books in which Harland kept a journal of sorts, not that I had ever read it. I picked it up with some trepidation. Even now I hesitated to intrude on his innermost thoughts, if that was what they were. I put that thought behind me, opened the book, and read these words in Harland's writing:

Research has shown that the hippocampus region of the brain is specifically responsible for processing memory. It is so called because its shape resembles that of the seahorse, in Latin called *hippocampus*. Coral reefs are a favourite habitat of the seahorse, and I sometimes like to think of human consciousness as one of those vast underwater cities whose fabric is accumulated from the skeletons of its builders: a necropolis which teems with life.

Here are massive blocks and towers of stone, hanging gardens of the most varied hues, purple, emerald and amethyst, which undulate and flicker beautifully in the transparent water. Fishes skim the galleries and avenues like flocks of birds, and the nooks and crannies are populated by a myriad of other species. What can the little seahorse know of this fantastic ecosystem? We cannot know. But we can say that its experience is a microcosm of the ongoing, thousands of years old saga that is the life of a coral reef, and which, like the human brain, we have yet to fully fathom.

The passage was familiar to me from somewhere. My heart gave a lurch as I realized that it had come from my abandoned novel, $X+Y=K$.

33

STAND AND UNFOLD YOURSELF

As Kilpatrick put the ring-binder in his briefcase he noticed a suitcase on the floor of the kneehole of the desk. He took off the suit jacket and laid it on the desk and then, with some difficulty, manipulated the mannequin until he had divested it of its trousers. He folded jacket and trousers neatly and put them in the suitcase, lifted both cases, went out the door, locked it, and made his way back to Hôtel Chopin. In Room 36 he took out the ring binder, opened it at random, and read these words:

When an organism interacts with an object, be it within body boundaries (for example, pain) or outside of them (for example, a landscape), it creates a narrative. This is true whether the object be perceived in the present moment, or recalled, for the past continues to influence our behaviour. The hippocampus is a vital structure in the mapping of multiple, concurrent stimuli. It receives signals related to activity in all sensory cortices, which arrive indirectly at the end of several projection chains with multiple synapses, and reciprocates signals via backward projections along the same chains. In plain speech, it is the instrument by which we assemble ourselves. A human being is a story-telling machine, and the self is a centre of narrative gravity.

Patients who have suffered severe lesions to the hippocampus lose the story of themselves: they are bereft of a past and of an anticipated future. They live in an eternal present, in which there is no elsewhere, no before, no after. Their wives, their husbands, their family and friends are constant and surprising strangers to them.

I see from your record, Mr Kilpatrick, that you are prone to bouts of amnesia: what we call transient global amnesia, specifically. It is a condition especially associated with migraine, and there can be little doubt that the electrical activity of migraine sometimes affects the hippocampus, causing temporary lapses in the processing of information. In these episodes – typically, they last for a few hours, usually less than a day – the otherwise entirely normal person is suddenly deprived of the records that have been recently added to the autobiographical memory. The immediate past, the past of the minutes just before, of the hours before, is a blank. Moreover, since our memory of the here and now also includes memories of the events we constantly anticipate – what I like to call memories of the future – it follows that the person struck by such amnesia will have no memory regarding what he intended for the minutes or the hours or days ahead. The idea of the future does not exist for him. Typically, the transient global amnesiac repeats the same questions: Where am I? What am I doing here? How did I come here? The case of K, if we might call you that for now, is especially fascinating, since it would seem that at times the narrative void caused by such attacks is bridged by K's alternative personality, the simulacrum K created as a child. Let us call this alter ego Mr X. When K's memory fails, X steps into the breach. Remember, X is not a simple stand-in, an ambitious understudy waiting in the wings for that moment when the leading man is laid low by some catastrophe, whether planned or accidental. Rather, it is as if Hamlet were replaced by Fortinbras, the thinker by the man of action. And *Hamlet* is a play about the narratives we create for ourselves, is it not? The parts we play? It concerns being or not being. That is the question. And the play starts with a question of identity. Act One, Scene One, line one: *Who's there?*

Kilpatrick read on, skimming here, dwelling on some passages there, trying to make sense of it. The book consisted of three sections: X, a first-person narrative; Y, a third-person narrative concerning a Gabriel Kilpatrick; and K, alternating between first-person and third-person as the protagonists of X and Y morph into someone called K and the events detailed in section X are revisited from his point of view. The last section seemed unfinished; or if it was finished, it was inconclusive. Common to all three sections was a fascination with memory, paranormal phenomena, surveillance, questions of identity, and the bombing campaign conducted by the Provisional IRA in Belfast in the latter decades of the twentieth century. For example:

Treading the glass grit in Corporation Square, Kilpatrick was reminded that it had been the scene of a bomb two days ago. There was some dispute as to whether the intended target was the Imperial Assurance offices or the Ulster Tea Importers next door. Whatever the case, the effects, as televised on that evening's *Scene Around Six*, had been spectacular. The planting of the device, in a Volkswagen estate car, had coincided with the arrival of a Hercules truck delivering a consignment of

Irish Breakfast tea. The occupants of the Hercules were forced at gunpoint to abandon their vehicle. The terrorists made their getaway in a second car, a Ford Capri. The Volkswagen exploded fifteen minutes later, causing extensive collateral damage to the structure of the immediate environment, including the Hercules truck and its cargo. Kilpatrick recalled the shudder of the camera's field of vision as it recorded car, truck and tea-chests disintegrating with a boom and whoosh, an atomic cloud of tea like starlings boiling upwards, sifting, settling on the twisted shrapnel already scattered like bits of art about the wide expanse of Corporation Square.

John Kilpatrick, reading this passage, realized that it was one of the many incidents – how many scores, how many hundreds? – he had forgotten. One lost count as one incident followed another in a series of amnesiac elisions. Yet everything was watched, overheard, recorded:

Electronic bugs – parasitic transmitters, Trojan Horse transistors, synaptic grafts or buds – were planted everywhere: in phones and door-handles and light fitments, spiked like hat-pins into the backs of hotel room curtains, masquerading as martini olives in hotel bars, lurking in the ceramic chain-pulls of hotel toilets. In smoke-filled back rooms the glint of an exposed floorboard nail was enough to invite suspicion. Cameras were concealed in smoke detectors, behind bar mirrors, and in bar optics, or were made to look like personal accoutrements: badges, buckles, brooches, bracelets, powder compacts, cigarette lighters. Taking into account that any conversation might be overheard, any covert action photographed, the players conducted conversations and actions accordingly, talking of this when they meant that, doing that instead of this.

And John Kilpatrick thought he remembered a conversation with John Bourne, who had playfully suggested that every new radio bought in Belfast was liable to be bugged: that it was both receiver and transmitter. But even if it were true, that wouldn't apply to Bourne's vintage EKO. So he had thought at the time. In hindsight, he wasn't so sure. One thing was certain: there was more to everything than met the eye.

34

A BENEFIT OF DOUBT

———•◆•———

I felt weak at the knees. I cleared a mound of debris from the old leather armchair where Harland would often sit to contemplate a work in progress; and, as I sat down and rolled a cigarette, I remembered how he'd offer me tobacco and papers, and I would roll one, pass him back the makings, and he would roll one too, the paper smeared with pigments from his hands; and when he lit up, the paper crackled and I thought of smoke being drawn into his lungs in a swirl of multicoloured particles. He'd look at the painting as I looked at it too; we would exhale together, and I wondered if we saw the same thing. I looked at the passage in his journal again. How could he have written these words of mine? for I had written them long after he had disappeared; he could not have read my book. Indeed, no-one but myself had read it. But then, looking at it again in Harland's chair, it seemed there was something not quite me about the style; it seemed like another voice, and then I remembered. I saw myself sitting at my desk with a 1950s book on neuroscience, transcribing bits of it into a notebook. The mystery was solved – obviously, he had read the book before I did, and he too had thought it worthwhile copying, for whatever purpose of his own. We had both indulged in a piece of appropriation. And yet a suspicion lingered that Harland had been watching me, for whatever purpose of his own.

I remembered the time I had gone to the toilet on the next landing down and had returned to see Harland standing by my jacket where it hung from a hook on the wall, going through the pockets. He had passed it off well – just admiring the material, old man, nice bit of tweed, where did you get it? And he drew my attention to flecks of heathery purple and sky blue and moss green, things I'd never really seen before, and I put the matter to one side. Until the next time, and the next, when he had let slip bits of information about my past or present circumstances, details of my life he could not have known; yet he always had a plausible story, or I would be loth to pursue the matter further, and I would once more put my suspicions to one side, giving him the benefit of the doubt. Only after he disappeared did I revisit these occasions, piecing together a narrative in hindsight, in which Harland was not all that he seemed, or all that I had taken him for.

I finished the cigarette and ground it into a drift of photocopied images. I went over and stood before the blemished dressing-table mirror. I looked like a ghost of myself. I opened a drawer at random. There was a box in the drawer. A box similar to the Japanese trick-box I had solved that morning, its surface covered by a labyrinth of marquetry, but a good deal bigger, some five inches by four by four. I looked at it closely but again I could see no joins. I worked it over in my hands for a good few minutes, but I knew it would take me forever to open it. I knew Harland had kept a hammer and chisel, and I found them on a shelf under a pile of paint-clotted rags. I took hammer and chisel to the box and smashed it open. Inside were half a dozen Polaroid photographs, and again my heart gave a lurch. A year or two before I met Harland I had bought a Land camera – it was still in my attic – and for some months I had experimented with a series of self-portraits taken in a mirror, which I would then distress with an array of implements – toothpicks, keys, old toothbrushes, swatches of needlecord, dragging and scumbling the still wet emulsion of the print to produce an altered image of myself, more psychologically accurate as I thought. I had signed and dated each on the back. These images were indubitably mine. I had shown them to no one: after meeting Harland, my work had seemed naive, mechanical and derivative compared to his painting, and I never mentioned them. But this discovery put a new complexion on how things stood between us.

As I pondered the matter, the drift of papers at my feet stirred as if in a breeze. I shivered. I recalled that Harland had taken the attic room when he heard it had been used for seances for some three years after the First World War by the Goligher Circle, a group of spiritualists centred around one Kathleen Goligher, a medium who claimed to be in contact with those who had passed over to the Other Side, the dead that is, who would communicate through her by a series of paranormal effects. Harland had first come across the case in a book called *The Psychic Structures at the Goligher Circle*, published in 1921 by William Jackson Crawford, then a lecturer in Engineering at Queen's University, Belfast, who had conducted a long series of elaborate tests on the Circle and was left in do doubt that the paranormal effects were genuine, that the world of the afterlife did indeed exist, and that those who dwelt there could indeed communicate to us by psychic rods extruded from the orifices of the medium's body. The rods tapped out messages in a primitive Morse, displaying a range of acoustic effects whose magnitude varied in intensity from barely audible ticks to sledgehammer blows. At times they sounded like gunshots. The seance room would be lit by a red lantern, said Harland, and here he quoted from Crawford's book: Why normal white light should prove destructive to physical phenomena is not fully understood, but an analogy with wireless helps to make it admissible. Light is the fastest vibration of the ether. Broadcasting practice demonstrates that the fast vibrations tend to nullify the slower vibrations of the radio waves as they are picked up by the wireless receiver. When the days are long and the sunlight intense, wireless reception drops down: this explains why broadcasts of cricket matches sometimes carry an accompanying charge of static, or fade from the air. With the oncoming of night reception improves again. It is probable that psychic vibrations are in the same position. The slowest light vibration is red, and its destructive effect far less. Sir William Crookes, testing the action of various light sources, found moonlight the least injurious to the phenomena. Says Crawford, said Harland. Of course it's a load of bunkum, old man, a matter of cheap conjuring tricks, said Harland, any amateur magician could do the same. And he took a coin from his pocket and made it disappear before my eyes. It's not the quickness of the hand that deceives the eye, it's your own brain that deceives yourself. We don't see what's there, we make up stories about what we think we see. And he would touch on the notorious fallibility of eyewitness accounts, which when taken together suggest that each onlooker has seen a different event.

I looked into the mirror remembering Cocteau's film *Orphée*, which I had first seen with John Harland, remembering how in that film, mirrors are the portals to the Underworld, and I thought of how I might glide through the mirror in the attic to a world where I might meet Harland once again, for all that he has been dead to me for many years. But when I looked at my watch I realised my time was short. It was nearly four o'clock and I, John Kilfeather, had another appointment to keep.

35

CONDUIT

By six o'clock of the evening after his experience in Rue du Sentier, John Kilpatrick had read all of $X+Y=K$, pausing here and there to take notes. The more he had read, the more had he seen uncanny resemblances between the Kilpatrick in the book and the Kilpatrick that was him. However, there were many more passages that did not tally with his own experience, and he recalled Blanqui's proposition that the universe contains infinite other, parallel worlds, and thus a myriad of other, endlessly doubled versions of ourselves, unbeknownst to each other and to ourselves. Perhaps $X+Y=K$ had drawn on some of those worlds, some of which corresponded to Kilpatrick's own. He also remembered that W.H. Auden had said that every man carries with him through life a mirror, as unique and impossible to get rid of as his shadow, and that Auden had then gone on to comment that we would be judged, not by the kind of mirror found on us, but by the use we have made of it. But what if another man's mirror were to cross ours, thought Kilpatrick, what would happen then? Would we become a third person? And what if other men, each with his mirror, crossed our paths? We would indeed then be many. These thoughts had crossed his mind the night before, when he had tried on the trousers of the suit he had found in Rue du Sentier. They too were a perfect fit. On further examination he found that, according to the tailor's label sewn into the lining of an inside pocket, the suit had been delivered to a Major R.E. Livingstone on the ninth of October 1966, Kilpatrick's eighteenth birthday, which made the suit forty-four years old. But it looked hardly worn; it might have been made yesterday.

Kilpatrick was wearing the suit now, in preparation for the evening to come. He had thought of meeting Bourne with some trepidation, but the garb lent him an air of quiet authority. For all that he did not yet know what part he would play in this unfolding drama, he felt like an actor who waits in the wings composing himself to deliver the words composed by another, nervous but confident that once he treads the boards the part will take him over. He imagined he might have rehearsed it in a mirror, drawing on affective memory, speaking to his reflection as he would to an audience, and he saw himself watching himself as if from a vantage point in the auditorium, the autumnal shades of the tweed he wore flickering in the spotlight as he suited the action to the word and the word to the action, everything happening as if déjà vu. The bedside telephone rang. A Monsieur Gordon awaited him in reception. Kilpatrick took a last look at himself in the dressing-table mirror, adjusted his tie, and went down to meet the man he was to meet.

Bonsoir, mon ami, said Gordon. *Bonsoir, mon ami*, said Kilpatrick. Under his Crombie overcoat Gordon was dressed in a grey Donegal tweed three-piece suit, and Kilpatrick remarked on it. Yes, thank you, nice bit of cloth you're wearing yourself.

1960s? Savile Row cut, I'd say, or maybe Conduit Street? Do as good a job in Conduit Street, half the price. Kilpatrick nodded. Gordon took a lapel between his thumb and finger. Nice hand, he said, pity about the little flaw there on the breast pocket. Kilpatrick had seen no flaw. Of course, they've done a great job on it, invisible menders, you wouldn't know it was there if you weren't looking for it. And of course, as I remarked before, we in the Profession are trained to look for these things. For all the world that looks like a mended bullet-hole, but of course you wouldn't know until the forensics had a good look at the fibres. Well, as it turns out, said Kilpatrick, its previous owner was a Major Livingstone, so you never know. H'm ... Livingstone, you say? said Gordon, there was a major of that name, one of our men, if I'm not mistaken, back in the sixties, wasn't a major at all of course, but played the part superbly. Until the Other Side rumbled him, that is. The Other Side? said Kilpatrick. Yes, said Kilpatrick, we're the Profession, and they're the Other Side. Kind of dialogue, if you like, one eye always watching the other. I take it you are one of us? Of course you are, though you might not even know it. Took some of us a while to get there, too. But you get there in the end. And then of course there's the Invisibles. The Invisibles? said Kilpatrick. Well, it's only a theory, more of a legend, said Gordon, but it's rumoured that whatever we and the Other Side do, there's another power at work, one which we cannot fathom, so that for all we know there is another narrative beyond the one we occupy. Perhaps the Invisibles, if they exist, insinuate themselves into the networks of surveillance created by us and the Other Side. We're all in the business of gathering information, you see, or disinformation. For the latter too is useful, since everything, fabricated or not, tells us something about the world we move in. Every contact leaves a trace. So we operate on the Exchange Principle. Are you with me? said Gordon. Kilpatrick nodded hesitantly. He remembered H.G. Wells' Invisible Man in a London fog, a greasy glimmer of a human shape, and again he saw himself as the Invisible Man trying on a player's mask and dark glasses in a theatrical costumier's in Drury Lane, peering at a grotesque image in a cheval mirror; or he was an onlooker to the Invisible Man's death on the pavement, the body slowly revealing itself as if infiltrated by a poison – first the little white nerves, a hazy grey sketch of a limb, then the glassy bones and intricate arteries, then the flesh and skin, first a faint fogginess and then growing rapidly dense and opaque. Finally he imagined himself scrutinizing the lost notebook which contained the invisibility formula, some of its pages washed out, the rest covered in a mixture of Russian, Greek, and mathematical symbols, full of unintelligible secrets.

We're in the business of knowing, said Gordon, for all that it's problematic to measure what we know against what we don't know. The Invisibles, if they exist, might well know things about us that we don't even know ourselves. But in any event it didn't take us long to know that you were one of us. That dream of yours, *Les structures sonores*, lovely title, that was enough in itself to convince us. The detail was uncanny, and we in the Profession depend on detail, for the devil is the detail, or what is it Flaubert says? *Le bon Dieu est dans le détail*. Two sides of the same coin. Nothing is unimportant. So we look at everything. Clouds, river deltas, root systems, coastlines, music, fluid turbulence, the fluctuations of the stock market, the movement of the crowd on a station concourse, raindrops trickling down a windowpane, all follow a pattern. Those kaleidoscopic shifts of which you spoke so eloquently. The assignation that is to us unexpected, the invitation coming seemingly from nowhere, has been dreamed of and initiated long in advance. Speaking of which, might I enquire about your encounter in Rue du Sentier? Kilpatrick couldn't remember if he had mentioned Rue du Sentier to Gordon. But he gave him the benefit of the doubt. He needed someone with whom to share his strange experience. So he told him the story. Yes, said Gordon, most interesting. The book especially, $X+Y=K$, you must take it to Bourne. He may be blind, but he can scan it in his own way, and his conclusions in these matters are always productive. A minute later Gordon and Kilpatrick left Hôtel Chopin, Kilpatrick carrying the book in his briefcase.

36

A LOST WORLD

I put the photographs and Harland's notebook into my briefcase. As I descended the staircase, my footsteps echoed in the stairwell as they had done many times in the past, often syncopated by his footsteps as he clattered down before or after me, and images of Harland flitted through my mind: Harland going through my pockets, Harland twiddling the knobs of the EKO radio as it gave out a fizz of static between bursts of unintelligible languages, Harland's smile as he gave me the Japanese box. When I reached the ground floor, the door of Federman's shop was locked. I was about to slip the key to the attic under his door when I thought better of it, and pocketed it. I emerged from 14 Exchange Place to find the bright October day had turned dark. Storm clouds had gathered overhead. As I stepped into the entry there was a flash of lightning followed by a roll of thunder. It began to pour rain. I stepped back into the vestibule for shelter, remembering a passage in $X+Y=K$ that had been prompted by a thunderstorm, or rather by Harland's recollection of a thunderstorm.

It began with his showing me a View-Master 3D disc of London, one of a dozen he had picked up in a junkshop, together with the accompanying viewer. One image showed the interior of the revolving restaurant of the Post Office Tower, which had closed, never to be reopened, after a terrorist bomb had exploded in the building on Hallowe'en, 1971. As I put the binocular device to my eyes I experienced again the dreamlike exaltation that comes when surrounding objects are shut out by the concentration of our whole attention, in which we seem to leave the body behind and sail into one strange scene after another, like disembodied spirits. In foreground of the View-Master image, a man held a cup about six inches from his pursed lips. Behind him a woman held a knife about to cut the bread roll she held in her other hand. A pre-school child held a menu, his mouth open as if pretending to read. A waitress's pencil was poised over an unwritten-on page. In this eternal moment, everyone seemed oblivious to the camera, except for one man standing with his back to the panoramic window, his head raised as if he had just that moment become aware of the photographer. Isn't there something eerie about him, said Harland, something which doesn't quite fit? You see the way nobody else seems aware of him, it's as if they're blind to him, or he's invisible. And indeed there was something incongruous about his presence among these conventionally dressed diners. I noted again the electric blue sharkskin suit, the snap-brim trilby pulled down over his forehead, the dark glasses turned in my direction so that I felt he was eyeing me directly through space and time.

As it happens, said Harland, I was in the restaurant the day before the bomb. A complete revolution took about twenty minutes, he said, and it occurred to me that the restaurant was itself a kind of timepiece, its movement like that of a minute hand, just about perceptible if you watched it closely. At one point I looked out and saw the twin towers of Wembley stadium glimmering on the horizon in a lake of mustard yellow under a purple sky. Thunder was in the air, and there was a biblical quality about the light that made the towers look like those of Nineveh or Babylon. I thought of the Turner landscapes I had seen that morning in the National Gallery. When I looked out again I found myself overlooking Westminster, almost face to face with Big Ben, as it were. It was fourteen minutes to one o'clock; as I looked at the clock face, the big hand leaped forward a fraction, and the sky above the clock tower was rent by a great flash. A split second later an almighty roll of thunder shook the windows. Rain poured down upon the city, which began to take on a curious underwater aspect, the streets appearing like the galleries of a coral reef, cars with their headlights switched on gliding like electric fish. It was quite exhilarating, said Harland. I felt like Captain Nemo in the observation chamber of the *Nautilus*. As Harland spoke I imagined the rain streaming down the windows, making them waver like shot silk, and I recognized the beginning of a migraine aura, I wrote in $X+Y=K$.

In fact I had not suffered from migraine since my teens but I had vivid memories of its effects. Migraine is not a simple headache. Rather, it is an aggregate of innumerable components, of which headache is only one; and it cannot be identified with any one symptom. Migraine headache is often described as a violent throbbing pain in one temple, but it can be located anywhere in the head, in the teeth, at the base of the nose, in the neck, as far down as the tip of the shoulder; in some cases, it may seem exteriorised, as in an extra phantom limb, or head. In extreme cases the migraineur sometimes feels he has an invisible body double. Common to many experiences of migraine is the aura, a term first applied to the sensory hallucinations immediately preceding certain epileptic seizures. The aura which precedes the migraine headache takes many forms, including deficits of speech and thought, muddled space-perception, and a variety of dreamy, delirious, and trancelike states. On closing the eyes, some patients experience a visual tumult or delirium, in which latticed, faceted and tessellated motifs predominate – images resembling mosaics, honeycombs, or Turkish rugs. These evanescent figments tend to be brilliantly luminous, coloured, highly unstable, and liable to sudden kaleidoscopic transformations. Occasionally these structures generate maps of enormous cities, as might be seen at night from a surveillance helicopter, with ring roads and radial spokes, illuminated, looking like giant spider-webs of light.

Sometimes the patient loses an entire half of his field of vision. It seems to him that half of the world has disappeared, or that it was never there in the first place, and he is gripped by a feeling of incomprehensible, overwhelming loss. Yet in other instances the experience is one of enlightenment. I remember when I was about thirteen or so, cycling along a country lane. Suddenly I feel as if I have lived this moment before, in the same place, though I have never travelled this road before. An extraordinary feeling of stillness comes upon me. This summer afternoon has always existed; I am arrested in an endless moment. I stop. My hands, my lips, my nose, my tongue are tingling. The sensation spreads through my whole body. Now it affects my eyes. As I look at the trees, the grass, the clouds, they exhibit a silent boiling. Everything is quivering and streaming upwards in a kind of ecstasy, the hum of crickets all around like a buzz of colour corresponding to the sound I hear. My body is vibrating to everything around me.

Standing in the vestibule of 14 Exchange Place, watching the rain pour down, I felt an overwhelming nostalgia. In my mind's eye I hovered above that scene of half a century ago, watching over the person I was then as if he were someone else, a thirteen-year-old boy who stands entranced by everything around him, not knowing or caring what will become of him in the years that lie ahead, for all that matters is now.

37

THE WINDING STAIR

The black limousine was waiting. Gordon and Kilpatrick seated themselves in the passenger cabin. The limousine drove off into the night. The book, said Gordon, let's call it X for now, open it. At random. Kilpatrick did as he was told. He opened the book at page 287. Read the first sentence, said Gordon. Kilpatrick read: In 1912 Edmund Edward Fournier d'Albe invented the optophone, which, by converting the light refracted from a page of printed matter into musical notes, enabled a blind person to read. Gordon clapped his hands together. Capital! he cried. You might say it is coincidence that we read about the blind on our way to see a blind man. But in our line of work there are no coincidences. You know the way you sometimes enter a library, in search of information; you've no idea where to begin looking, and yet something directs you to a particular shelf, to take down a particular book, for no good reason as far as you can tell, but it turns out to be the very book you need. And often the first sentence you read is just what you've been looking for, though you didn't know it until then. Some call this phenomenon the Library Angel. But there are those amongst us who prefer to ascribe it to the work of the Invisibles. We call such passages of text Unseens. As it happens, John Bourne has developed a modified optophone for his painting. Essentially a simple concept, you translate colour wavelength into sound wavelength, I don't know the exact correspondences, say the note C is white, F-sharp black, G red, and so on through the spectrum. So you can see, or rather hear, that a work by John Bourne is a musical experience as well as a visual one. And of course the converse is true, you can translate sound into colour. Come to think of it, you could translate anything into anything. Scent, taste, whatever. You could have an aromaphone, for example. Anyway, Bourne's working on a series at present, Bach's *The Art of Fugue*.

Contrapunctus XIV, said Kilpatrick. Yes? said Gordon. Well, said Kilpatrick, the café where I met Freddy Gabriel, it was playing on the sound system, it's the last movement of *The Art of Fugue*, Freddy came in on the last few bars. Did he now? said Gordon. I wouldn't put it past Freddy to have engineered it, set it up as a conversation piece. Whatever the case, it goes to show us yet again that there's no such thing as coincidence, said Gordon. Everything's part of a larger narrative. We're all trying to make sense of what we see, but of course the visual input and the means of processing it are extraordinarily complex, multiple feedback loops at every stage of the hierarchy. Let's say there's a black box at every stage. But you open the black box, and what does it contain? Why, a whole labyrinth of smaller black boxes. So we sort out what's what by going through a series of iterations, eliminating those that don't fit the parameters as we think of them. We seem to see things in a split second, but there's any number of other split seconds behind that one. It's as if each of us is hallucinating all the time and what we call perception involves merely selecting the one hallucination that best matches the current input, a plausible narrative if you like. Makes sense to us, anyway. So let me posit a little scenario.

A writer, let us call him K, said Gordon, is spending a sojourn in Paris. He is researching a book about Paris which will include extracts from books set in Paris, matching them to the relevant locations. It is an enterprise of some complexity, for sometimes the correspondence between extract and location is tenuous, especially in works of fiction; or the location has changed, or has been redeveloped beyond all recognition. The Les Halles quarter is a case in point. No matter. K enjoys these investigations of how things appear in books and how they appear in the world, sometimes imagining himself to walk in the footsteps of a fictional character and seeing the world through his eyes. He could be in a motion picture, complete with incidental music: a Bach fugue, say, for all that K's memory of the piece is impressionistic and diverges somewhat from an actual performance. No matter. In his mind they set the atmosphere. For a while things go unremarkably. He visits places he has visited in the past, and loses himself in places he has never been. He describes these peregrinations in a notebook. One day he sees a man who bears an uncanny resemblance to someone who once played an important role in K's life. He gives the man a name, John Bourne. The man vanishes. One thing leads to another ... But we have arrived at our location, said Gordon. He pushed a button on the armrest and it slid open to reveal a radio. *L'oiseau chante avec ses doigts*, he said into it, and the radio replied, *Et l'homme chant avec ses ailes.*

The limousine came to a halt by a piece of wasteland. It was a quarter of Paris unfamiliar to Kilpatrick. As in a bomb site from some war or other, tall ruined buildings stood at one end of a skyline overlooking an area of rusted metal and broken masonry. The two men picked their way through the rubble. Here, said Gordon. He scuffled a few bricks out of the way to reveal a cast-iron manhole cover. Kilpatrick could not read the writing, but it looked ancient. Gordon produced two long iron T-shaped bars from his pocket. He gave one to Kilpatrick. Takes two to shift it, he said. Put the key in the slot, like this, he said, and he did so. Kilpatrick followed suit. They heaved together, and the iron lid came off not without struggle. It clanked heavily when they lowered it to the ground. Gordon replaced the keys and produced an electric torch from his pocket. I'll light the way, he said, and Kilpatrick could see in the yellow beam a series of iron rungs going down until they disappeared into darkness. He followed Gordon down the ladder, rung after rung, until they landed in a chamber lined with shelves on which were arrayed human skulls. Old catacombs, said Gordon, there's a veritable labyrinth of them down here. We go this way. He opened a door with another key from his pocket and they entered a winding passageway. A winding stair. Yet another door, another key. Nearly there, said Gordon. They came to another door again. Gordon halted before it, switched off his torch, and the door swung open of its own accord. Take my hand, and watch the step, said Gordon, as they stepped down into a room that was completely dark.

Welcome, said a voice, and Kilpatrick knew he had heard the voice before, not the voice but the shadow of a voice he knew behind this older one. Scenes from the past of that voice flickered before his eyes and he heard John Bourne talking of the music of Bach, of the structure of *cannabis sativa*, of the painting of Francis Bacon, of Glenn Gould's consumption of pharmaceutical drugs and Francis Bacon's passion for gambling, of Hermes the God of Chance, of the one hundred billion neurons in the human brain ... Identify yourselves, said the voice. Paul Gordon, said Gordon. And the other? said the voice. Gordon nudged Kilpatrick. John Kilpatrick, said Kilpatrick. There was a pause of a second that seemed an eternity.

Long time no see, said John Bourne.

38

THE FOUND HOUR

As I stood in the vestibule of 14 Exchange Place, lost for a moment in a lost time, I heard the Albert Clock tolling the hour as it had done, hour by hour, for the fugitive protagonist of *Odd Man Out*. I counted three strokes. I looked at my watch. It read four. Spring forward, Fall back. I realised I'd forgotten to turn the clock back last night, the last Sunday in October, Hallowe'en as it happened. Today was All Saints' Day. Then I remembered that the same thing had happened to me when I wrote in the missing notebook, when was it? One or two or three years ago, years that had passed in a blur so that it seemed to me only yesterday. I could hardly tell one year in the past decade or two from another; as we age, subjective time accelerates. The summers of our childhoods seem to stretch forever; now they seem over before they have begun. On the other hand, when we are abroad, away from our routine existence, time seems to slow; every day is full of incident, new things to see, and a week seems a month. And indeed, the three days of my enforced absence from home, when I was abroad as it were, seemed much longer than that. As it was, I had an hour to kill. I set my watch to three o'clock, the Omega likewise, sat down on the stairs, and took Harland's notebook from my briefcase. It was still pouring rain outside.

I opened the notebook at random and glanced at the handwriting that was still familiar to me after all these years, a formal miniscule out of character with his ostensibly open face, and the broad strokes and swirls of his painting. I had remarked on it to Harland once and he said he had modelled it on the tiny handwriting of Walter Benjamin. He said it disciplined his thoughts, and he then showed me a book he was reading, written by a Lisa Fittko, who had helped Benjamin escape through the Pyrenees. Benjamin had spent some time in Lourdes before embarking on that fatal journey. The hotels and boarding houses of the town, usually catering almost exclusively to Catholic pilgrims, were packed with refugees, many of whom were Jewish: one of those bizarre displacements that happen in times of war. It was September 1940. Benjamin had already tried and failed to escape through Marseilles, a city in whose apocalyptic atmosphere, said Fittko, there were new stories every day about absurd escape attempts; plans involving fantasy boats and fictitious captains, visas for countries not found on any map, and passports issued by nations which no longer existed. She referred to Benjamin as 'Old Benjamin' – she didn't know why, since Benjamin was only forty-eight or so, she said, the age that Harland and I were at the time, and we certainly didn't think of ourselves as old. Yet the photograph of Benjamin in the book showed a man who looked much older and wiser than us, wearing wire-rimmed glasses, his hair rising from the high brow in a shock of convoluted waves shot with grey, the very image of an intellectual.

Benjamin had a heart condition, and his ascent through the mountains was arduous. He was carrying a heavy, black leather briefcase which contained his new manuscript. Timing himself

187

with his gold watch, he would stop every ten minutes to rest for one minute. At the time Fittko had only a vague idea of Benjamin's reputation, and to her the briefcase was a superfluous burden, 'a monstrosity'. But he would not be parted from it. He dared not lose it, the manuscript was more important than himself, he said. Of course we all know what happened then, said Harland, Benjamin took an overdose of morphine when he arrived in Portbou, and the manuscript vanished. Years later scholars searched high and low in Portbou for the manuscript, descending even into the catacombs of the town. But it was never found, though the briefcase was entered in the death register, with the notation, 'and some papers of an unknown content'. So the briefcase became a relic made all the more potent by its disappearance. There's another twist not mentioned by Fittko, said Harland. Benjamin was buried not as a Jew but as a Christian, in the Catholic cemetery of Portbou; the death certificate was made out in the name of Doctor Benjamin Walter, and the parish records contain a receipt for payment of a Mass for the dead man's soul, and the rent of the cemetery niche. So in death Benjamin became someone else, a reversal of his name, said Harland.

Death is the sanction for everything that the storyteller can tell, Benjamin has written elsewhere. And I reflected, in this hour granted to me by an arbitrary act of temporal authority, on Benjamin's saying that Marcel Proust was most aware of his approaching death when he was writing, as the syntax of his prose enacted, step by step, parenthesis by parenthesis, his fear of suffocating through asthma: a counterpoint of ageing and remembering, not what he experienced, but what he recollected.

A fugue in other words, left necessarily incomplete by the author's death; Proust, when alive, and dying, was constantly revising in the light of what he had written since, and there could be no end to the enterprise. And when Benjamin suggests that Proust's celebrated involuntary memory is much closer to forgetting than to remembering, I think of how little remains to me of my times with Harland, from sober encounters to drunken, ecstatic nights when we lived life to the full, whose details were almost entirely forgotten by us the next day, and faded into nothingness thereafter. When Proust in a well-known passage described the hour that was most his own, he did it in such a way that everyone can find in it his own existence. We might almost call it an everyday hour, a lost twittering of birds, a breath drawn at the sill of an open window. And I remember sunlight falling through stained glass windows at a certain hour of an afternoon, what year it is I do not know, and sunlit bubbles rising through a glass of beer as Harland raises the glass to me and to himself. What did I, Kilfeather, really know of Harland? I did not even know where he came from. When I would hazard a question as to his previous existence, the answers were always ambiguous or vague. We lived in a present of which I remember only some fragments. I see him painting me, or painting himself, and can no longer remember which was which.

It is late at night, and it is dark, but a shaft of moonlight falls through the dormer window of the studio, illuminating Harland's pale face as he draws on the Black Rose, then hands it to me. We listen to the Albert Clock toll the hour. Twelve strokes. Ask not for whom the bells tolls, I said. Not quite, said Harland, *never send to know* for whom the bell tolls, it tolls for thee. John Donne,

'Meditation XVII'. He got up from the chair, lifted a book from a shelf, and riffled through the pages. Ah yes. And just before that, we have this passage: All mankind is of one author, and is one volume; when one man dies, one chapter is not torn out of the book, but translated into a better language; and every chapter must be so translated; God employs several translators; some pieces are translated by age, some by sickness, some by war, some by justice; but God's hand is in every translation, and his hand shall bind up all our scattered leaves again for that library where every book shall lie open to one another. One John to all the others, said John Harland.

39

THE RALEIGH BICYCLE

———•◆•———

Before Kilpatrick knew it, Paul Gordon vanished. A dim light came on and Kilpatrick saw John Bourne for the first time in, what was it? ten, twenty, thirty years. He was seated in a high-backed armchair. He seemed scarcely aged. The grey Prince of Wales check suit he was wearing was one that Kilpatrick knew from before. Bourne was wearing a brown fedora hat with the brim pulled over his eyes and he wore a wry smile. Seeing is believing, is it not, said Bourne. You have been looking for me, and what do you see? Something that I always was, albeit that for some time I did not know that thing. And who are you? he said to Kilpatrick. I am John Kilpatrick, said Kilpatrick. That remains to be seen, said John Bourne. We come to everything in time, and what is time? As John Donne would have it, is it in 'Meditation XIV'? If we consider time to be motion, then it has three stations, past, present and future; but the first and last of these is not, because one is not now and the other is not yet; and that which you call present, is not now the same that it was, when you began to call it so. So we flit eternally into the future, infinitesimal split second by second. In like manner a hierarchy of angels can dance upon a pinpoint. What are you then? said Kilpatrick. I am you, I am anybody, said Bourne. Before I lost my sight I was blind, and now I see. I see the legions that are each of us hovering about us as if watching over us, for all that they are blind to our existence. Only I have retrospection for them, and that enables me to see. But let me show you who you are. Bourne raised himself and gestured to a cheval mirror that stood beside him. What do you see? said Bourne. Kilpatrick walked over to the mirror and regarded himself. I see John Kilpatrick, he said, the man I am. Well and good, said Bourne, but what do you see behind you in the mirror? I see a door, said Kilpatrick. To see you we must go and open it, said Bourne.

They walked to the door which led them to a large bright chamber. Welcome to the Memory Palace, said Bourne. He gestured to the shelves and alcoves which lined the room, each of them filled with a miscellanea of objects. Third shelf, top right, you'll see a tin toy submarine, a little rusted. That was Stanley, who thought himself someone else until he touched the toy, or it him. This alcove here on the left, a bookcase made out of an orange crate, you can still smell the oranges, that was Burgess, same story. He swept his arm around the room. Kilpatrick saw an old Clydesdale radio, a red and white enamel tricycle, a pottery owl, a cricket bat, a cast-iron mangle, a frayed blanket. There were hundreds of objects arrayed in no apparent order. I know where everything is, said Bourne. All the things you see here I see too, because I link them to the people, and their stories of who they were, and who they might have been. And I see the things too because I have touched them all, and they me, and I know their aura. For all of them were loved deeply in their day, and were alive to them that loved them. So let me show you who you were, because you are what you always were. Next room.

There you are. Raleigh tourer, 1959 model, Sturmey-Archer gears, said Bourne, I think you'll find it all in order. Kilpatrick's heart stopped for a second as he looked at the bicycle. He recognized it instantly in the deep blue enamel livery set off by the whitewall tires, and the proud worn leather of the seat, and the butterfly curve of the handlebars, everything about it that he so loved, and he was thirteen again. What do you see? said Bourne. I see a boy of thirteen, said Kilpatrick. It is a beautiful June morning with fair weather clouds scudding in the blue sky and I am riding my bicycle down a country lane. Suddenly I feel as if I have lived this moment before, in the same place, though I have never travelled this road before. An extraordinary feeling of stillness comes upon me. This summer afternoon has always existed. Everything is quivering and streaming upwards in a kind of ecstasy, my body is vibrating to everything around me, said Kilpatrick, and I am unbearably happy because in this endless moment I do not know who I am because I am everything around me.

So it is written in the book, said Bourne, the book of all our lives. What is your name? Kilpatrick hesitated. The bicycle, man, look at the bicycle, said Bourne. And then Kilpatrick knew who he was. He turned the bicycle round and there, in white paint on the seat tube in a boy's careful schoolboy script, was written J. Kilfeather. So now you know, said Bourne, as I once got to know. You know what got me? No, not the cricket bat. I played that one well at the time. Top left shelf, seventh object along. Kilfeather found himself staring at pair of navy women's court shoes, late 1940s style, stacked heel. My mother's shoes, said Bourne, I wore them one Hallowe'en when I was what? four or five, and I clattered around in the dark in them and a long dress, seeing fireworks go off all around me. Funny the way things move you. You suffer from migraine in your teens? Kilfeather nodded. A lot of us did, said Bourne, with others it's epilepsy. It's all in the aura, don't you see? It changes the world for you, or rather it changes you for the world, because the world is always what it is no matter what. When I realized that I really started to paint. The other thing was just something I did for the Other Side unbeknownst to myself, when they put the fugue on me, just like they did on you. The fugue? said Kilfeather. You know your classic fugue, said Bourne. Yes, said Kilfeather, from *fugere*, to flee. Yes, said Bourne, variant of temporary global amnesia, person thinks he's someone else, often found in migraineurs, normally it only lasts a matter of months or weeks, but the Other Side found a way of inducing it to last for years. It was only when I was born again that I remembered the chair, the helmet with the electrodes, like one of those hair salon hairdryers. Not that it was unpleasant. Far from it, something like sinking into black velvet. I heard a voice in my head speaking of green fields. Then I was gone, and John Browne the printer woke up in another city as John Bourne the painter. The Other Side don't like their alters to be too disjunctive. I kept the name Bourne, a bit more class to it, don't you think? Though you may call me Browne. So there you are: you're an alter too. But there's a twist to the plot. The Other Side have planted another alter in Belfast, a John Kilfeather who is masquerading as you, unbeknownst to himself. Not to mention the fact that he's introduced a character dangerously close to me, courtesy of the Other Side again, calls him John Harland. We must redress the balance, said John Browne, and Kilfeather knew he was speaking the truth. What must I do? he said.

First we must kit you out, said Browne. The suit is excellent, of course, what an operation though, overkill if you ask me, our people in Belfast had the neighbourhood closed down with a bomb scare for three days just to get into the house. You won't need the book, we've already been through it with a fine-tooth comb. Interesting propositions if fanciful at times, doesn't tell us anything we don't already know. In any event it's a copy, we needed the fake Kilfeather to have the original for continuity purposes, and of course you will have access to that when the time comes. The only thing you really need is the gun. The gun? said Kilfeather, and Browne handed him the Luger pistol.

40

REVELATION

———◆◆◆———

The rain was still pouring down from an apocalyptic sky. I heard the Albert Clock strike the half-hour, the same reverberating note that struck me so many times over the years, giving me that next half-hour of grace before I saw the person whom I was to meet, half an hour in which the words would come to me unbidden as I wrote them down; and I remembered countless other times writing ecstatically in a notebook, whether under an awning in the pouring rain or on the sunlit terrace of a café, scribbling for months, for years, circling round a theme that only gradually discloses itself, pages covered in words, arrows leading back to other words, words crossed out, addenda, corrigenda, pages flickering behind the page I write in now. I flicked through the previous entries.

It seems like a dream, or so it seems now when I look back at it, I had written days ago, a week ago, a month ago. The entry bore no date. Only now am I waking up to it, in a manner of speaking, said the entry. What led to it? It all depends how far back one goes. Did it begin here, in this blink of an eyelid, or elsewhere, in another? So it was written.

Contrapunctus XIV, I had written. Journeys in fractal land are arduous. Mandelbrot: 'length' is not something that can be meaningfully specified. Mandelbrot quotes Edmund Whymper on mountaineering: It is worthy of remark that ... fragments of rock ... often represent the characteristic form of the cliffs from which they have been broken.

I am wearing a pair of Oxford brogues by 'K' shoes of Kendal, 1960s vintage, bought on eBay, I had written. I looked down at my feet. I was wearing them now. They had been barely worn yet when I put them on I could feel the imprint of another's foot upon the insole, and I wondered who had walked in them before me. Kendal in the Lake District, I had written, Wordsworth country, the poet striding for miles up hill down dale as the words came to him unbidden and he cried them aloud with every step he took. There was a time when meadow, grove, and stream, the earth, and common sight, to me did seem apparell'd in celestial light, the glory and the freshness of a dream.

I paused from my writing and looked up at the sky. The rain had ceased and a sun pale as the moon drifted through the clouds. I felt that sensation of a migraine aura steal over me once again. The brickwork of the building opposite was charged with pattern, brick and mortar interstices undulating like a piece of music. I closed my book, took up my briefcase and walked out into the street, spellbound by everything I saw, the gutter heaving like a river in spate, the manhole covers under my feet like heraldic shields laid down by a forgotten empire. When I looked up I saw domes and cupolas, battlements and parapets gleaming on the skyline of the city under the leaden clouds, and my route now seemed preordained from some distant epoch. A car-horn sounded ceremonially and my whole being shimmered with the knowledge that the atoms of my brain had been forged aeons ago in the stars, billions of atoms forming dense thickets of neurons and transmission cables endlessly communicating, more active often in sleep than in waking life.

I walked towards my destination along the route that I had taken for many years, and with every footstep I took, I watched the city unfolding herself in all the beauty and the glory of her detail. And I heard the words of John the Divine, And the twelve gates of the city were twelve pearls; every gate was of one pearl; and the street of the city was pure gold, as it were transparent glass. I walked among the people invisible to them, the apparition of these faces in a crowd, and I looked upon them, and I knew these nameless ones for all they knew me not. What was my name? Where was I coming from? Where was I going? I was this John, and that John, and the other John, and I was everyone and everything around me. I was yet to write the book in which all would be revealed, these lives of which I was the author, but now my path was clear, I knew the words would come when the time came, and I was filled with exaltation.

Before I knew it I was sitting under an awning outside the Morning Star. I ordered a Pernod with ice, a jug of water on the side. I poured water into the spirit and watched it slowly change from clear to cloud. The little miracle never failed to please me. I rolled a cigarette and took out my notebook. I lit the cigarette and took a sip of Pernod. I checked my watch and then thought to check the Omega I was to show my client. Both were almost exactly in synch, the second hand of the Wittnauer sweeping a little in advance of the Omega as if leading it on into the future. Beautiful watch the Omega, I was loth to part with it, maybe I could fob him off with the promise of something he would think better, a Rolex which if not exactly fake had been compromised by what they call reconditioning, covers a few sins invisible to the untrained eye. I put the Omega back in the briefcase and wrote in the notebook: I am Alpha and Omega, the beginning and the ending, which is, and which was, and is to come. As I did so there was a flash of lightning followed by an almighty peal of thunder, and it started to pour rain again. It dripped from the awning spattering the words I had just written; but no matter, I moved to a more sheltered spot, taking with me my accoutrements of drink, tobacco and briefcase, and continued to write the first words that came into my mind. I heard them spoken from afar and I was merely setting down that which was dictated by another, my pen struggling to keep pace as word came after word. What thou seest, write in a book, said the voice.

My roll-up had gone out and when I made to relight it, I glanced up and saw a figure sitting in the shadows under the awning. He too was drinking Pernod, an unusual enough occurrence in Belfast. Paris, yes, but not here. His face was obscured by the brim of his brown fedora, but all the same there was something in his bearing that looked familiar to me. Nice suit he was wearing too, a brown tweed not unlike the one I had looked for just before I went out. I could do something with this, I thought, but put it to one side for future reference as I kept writing: And I went unto the angel, and said to him, give me the little book. And he said unto me, Take it, and eat it up; and it shall make thy belly bitter, but it shall be in thy mouth sweet as honey. So absorbed was I in writing, I did not see him coming. When I looked up he was sitting before me, his face still hidden by his hat. He set a briefcase on the table. His hands were trembling.

He raised his head and looked at me. There was a flash of lightning and I saw myself looking at myself. My heart gave a great leap. Who was I? Everything went blank.

41

THE MISSING NOTEBOOK

This too is you, said John Browne. And Kilfeather held again the replica Luger pistol he had held as a child, made of convincingly heavy metal but fed by little pink plastic cartridges rather than the real thing, and he was transported back to a time when he killed and was killed to pass the time, boy soldiers throwing up their arms theatrically then falling and rolling down a grassy ridge in a simulation of dying, rising again to fight again, over and over through a long summer's day. You don't need real, said Browne, the man has a heart condition, he's on a cocktail of drugs, atoravastatin, clopidogrel, and the Lord knows what else. Heavy smoker too. All it takes is a shock to the system. More likely than not the mere sight of you will be enough to tip the blood pressure over the edge. Oh, and you'll need a hat to hide your face, more impact when you reveal yourself. Here, take mine, said Browne, and he took off his fedora and placed it on Kilfeather's head. It was a nice fit. The sweatband was cold against his forehead. You've always wanted to do that, said Browne, haven't you? Wear my hat. But you were too shy to ask. And Kilfeather knew he spoke the truth.

About quarter of an hour or so, and then we're all set. We've set the time parameters so that you make the rendezvous just before the fake Kilfeather. While we're waiting I thought you'd like to see my new work, *Contrapunctus XIV*, or hear it indeed. This way, said Browne, extending his arm. He led Kilfeather to another room. *Voilà*. Kilfeather saw before him a large panel some six feet by three. It was nothing like the work of the man he had known as John Bourne. Imagine a hundred Mark Rothkos miniaturized and patterned like a musical score, he thought, lozenges and rectangles of earth tones and purples and deep blues and burnt oranges fading and blurring into one another, intersected by diagonal slashes in brighter tones, shimmering against the lower octaves, light sounding on deep. You need the wand to get the full effect, said the man who now was Browne, and he handed him what looked like a long slim truncheon of crystal. Wave it about as your fancy takes you, said Browne, point it at the bits that engage you, and then look for bits that never caught your eye in the first place. The 'on' button is here. Kilfeather switched it on and immediately heard a deep melodious humming. He waved the wand before the painting and the painting emitted a music that was glassy at first, and then like wind-chimes, and then like the deep sounds of a forest floor. He waved it another way and he heard the fair weather clouds drifting across a June morning sky. He waved it again and he heard the moaning of the wind in the trees and the sad sound of November rain dripping through bare trees and it seemed to him that the permutations could go on forever. There's never enough time, said Browne gently, for we only have so much time on earth, but when we depart there are always the others whom we might have been and are, because all of us are no one but each other. He took the wand from him.

Now you you'll need the Changing Room, said Browne. The changing room? said Kilfeather. Well, you don't need to change the outfit, that's all as it should be, but you need to go through the portal, that's the mirror, antique Venetian, mercury backing, said Browne. And I nearly forgot, you need a little drug to smooth the process, induces an aura, puts the neurons properly in synch. Remember those magic mushrooms we used to eat? He produced a miniature Pernod bottle from his pocket. Same psychoactive ingredient, synthesized, the natural stuff is too unpredictable for our purposes, we've got this tailored to your body weight and psychological profile, bespoke psilocybin as it were, you'll find it does the trick. Here's the procedure, said Browne. When you come out the other side you must proceed immediately to the Morning Star bar. You'll know how to get there. Sit outside, under the awning. Your man will arrive in five minutes or so. Wait until he is settled, then confront him. You may or not need the gun. I'll leave that up to you. It's all very straightforward. *Faîtes simple.* This way. He walked over to a curtain and twitched it to one side. *Voilà.* Put the pistol in your briefcase. And this notebook, you might find it useful when the time comes. Passport in your name, ditto. Drink the drug, said Browne. Kilfeather did as he was told. He felt the effects almost immediately. The cubicle was nicely furnished, 1950s rose trellis wallpaper, and as he looked at it the roses began to shimmer. He looked at the mirror. The surface of the glass was like black ice with a faint pinpoint of light at its centre. He went over and touched the glass and it was cold and hard as ice. Takes a few minutes more to warm up, said Browne.

When the time was right, Kilfeather stepped up to the mirror, extending his hands like a swimmer about to take the plunge, and as his fingertips reached the dark glass it parted like liquid mercury to swallow him bit by bit until he vanished down a deep dark well. He felt himself going down for a long time, falling through time as he thought of it, second by infinitesimal second, until he emerged from the mirror in the attic of 14 Exchange Place into a drift of photocopied images, images he knew from before. He descended the stairs into the entry, turned the corner into Donegall Street, and was sitting under the awning of the Morning Star within a matter of two or three minutes. It was pouring rain when he saw the man sit down under the awning and when he approached him there was a flash of lightning and both men saw each other clearly for a split second.

A man came to some time after, not knowing who he was. On reflection he realised he must have had a bout of transient global amnesia. He remembered the aura. There was a briefcase at his feet. He opened it and took out a toy gun, a passport and Muji A6 notebook. He would think about the gun later. He opened the passport and looked at the photograph. He did not think it looked like him compared to how he looked now. He thought it must have been taken some time ago, when he was not the man he was now. He read the name on the passport. So that was him, then. He opened the notebook at an entry that was spattered with rain, and as he read these words he thought he might be reading a key to a book he had had in mind to write for how many years he could not remember: It begins or began with a missing notebook, an inexpensive Muji A6 notebook, with buff card covers and feint-ruled pages. On the inside cover is written, If found, please return to John Kilfeather, 41 Elsinore Gardens,

Belfast BT15 3FB Northern Ireland, United Kingdom, Europe, The World.

Again a flash of lightning: he needed to write. He looked in the briefcase and found a pen. Nice vintage Waterman, marbled celluloid. He unscrewed the cap and began to write. The pen suited his hand well, it could have been his own pen, and it wrote first time, the writing both familiar and foreign. He kept on writing. The writing kept on, words appearing from nowhere.

ACKNOWLEDGEMENTS

The author and publisher gratefully acknowledge permission to include the following copyright material

BENJAMIN, WALTER, extracts from 'Stamp Dealer', *One-Way Street and Other Writings* (first published as 'The Work of Art in the Age of Mechanical Reproduction') Penguin Books 2008. This selection and translation first published in Penguin Modern Classics 2009. Translation copyright © J.A. Underwood, 2008, 2009.

BENJAMIN, WALTER, reprinted by permission of the publisher from *The Arcades Project* by Walter Benjamin, translated by Howard Eiland and Kevin McLaughlin, pp. 84, 112, 114, Cambridge, Mass.: The Belknap Press of Harvard University Press, Copyright © 1999 by the President and Fellows of Harvard College. Originally published as *Das Passagen-Werk*, edited by Rolf Tiedemann, Copyright © 1982 by Suhrkamp Verlag.

BENJAMIN, WALTER, *Walter Benjamin's Archive: Images, Texts, Signs,* translated by Esther Leslie (Verso, London, 2007), reproduced by kind permission of Verso Books.

BENJAMIN, WALTER, reprinted by permission of the publisher from *Walter Benjamin: Selected Writings, Volume 1, 1913–1926,* edited by Marcus Bullock and Michael W. Jennings, pp. 478, 479, 491 Cambridge, Mass.: The Belknap Press of Harvard University Press, Copyright © 1996 by the President and Fellows of Harvard College. Originally published as *Das Passagen-Werk*, edited by Rolf Tiedemann, Copyright © 1982 by Suhrkamp Verlag.

COCTEAU, JEAN, *Mon premier voyage: tour du monde en 80 jours* (Editions Gallimard, 1936); *Round the World Again in 80 Days*, translation by Stuart Gilbert, 1937 (Tauris Parke, 2000) © Editions Gallimard 1936, reproduced by kind permission of Editions Gallimard.

FROST, ROBERT, *The Notebooks of Robert Frost*, edited by Robert Faggen (Harvard University Press, 2007), reproduced by kind permission of the Estate of Robert Lee Frost.

MCKEE, DAVID, extract from 'Spaceman', *The Extraordinary Adventures of Mr Benn* by David McKee (Hodder Children's Books, 2009) first published in the UK by Hodder Children's, an imprint of Hachette Children's Books, 338 Euston Road, London, NW1 3BH.

MODIANO, PATRICK, *Rue des boutiques obscures* (Editions Gallimard, 1978), © Editions Gallimard 1978; *La petite bijou* (Editions Gallimard, 2001), © Editions Gallimard 2001, reproduced by kind permission of Editions Gallimard.

SACKS, OLIVER, *Migraine* (Picador, 1995), the information on migraines owes much to Sacks' publication.

SHERRIFF, ROBERT C. and F.L. GREEN, 'Odd Man Out', *Three British Screenplays*, edited by Roger Manvell (Methuen, 1950), reproduced with permission of Curtis Brown Group Ltd, London on behalf of the Estate of R.C. Sherriff. Copyright © R.C. Sherriff, 1947.